CHASE

The voice on the telephone was tense and ugly. 'You messed in where you had no right messing . . . I just want to tell you that it doesn't end here. I'll deal with you, Mr Chase, once I've researched your background and have weighed a proper judgment on you. Then, once you've been made to pay, I'll deal with the whore, the Allenby girl.'

'Deal with?' Chase asked.

'I'm going to kill you and her, Chase.'

Also available in Star

**WHISPERS
NIGHT CHILLS
PHANTOMS
SHATTERED**

CHASE

Dean R. Koontz

A STAR BOOK
Published by
the Paperback Division of
W.H. ALLEN & Co. PLC.

A Star Book
Published in 1984
by the Paperback Division of
W.H. Allen & Co. PLC
44 Hill Street, London W1X 8LB

First published in the United States of America by
Random House, Inc., 1972

Typeset by Phoenix Photosetting, Chatham
Printed and bound in Great Britain by
Anchor Brendon Ltd, Tiptree, Essex

ISBN 0 352 31489 3

For Bob Hoskins

... had appreciated Mr Dwyer hope you had it entertain ...

Preface

Chase was my first suspense novel, written when I was twenty-five, published when I was twenty-six. Like *Shattered*, which Star Books brought back into print last year, *Chase* was originally published by Random House under the name K. R. Dwyer, a pseudonym I no longer employ.

This is the first paperback edition in the United Kingdom, and I am delighted that it bears my own by-line, at last. These two novels have been widely translated, published, and reprinted, but because they are among my favourites of my own books, I have always regretted hiding behind the Dwyer identity. Now, that unhappy situation is remedied.

Although *Chase* and *Shattered* are self-contained novels that do not share any story or character elements, they *do* share some thematic components and can be viewed as a two-book exploration of social and psychological conditions in the United States during the early 1970s. At that time, the country was shaken by anti-war protests and civil disobedience (some of it not so civil), and the atmosphere was redolent of paranoia. Benjamin Chase (in *Chase*) and Alex Doyle (in *Shattered*) both learn to distrust authority; they both come to believe that politics – whether of the left or the right – offers no solutions; and they are redeemed by their acceptance of self-reliance as the greatest of all virtues.

Most of all, *Chase* is a thriller. Both I and the late, unlamented Mr Dwyer hope you find it entertaining.

Dean Koontz
Orange, California
1983

CHASE

One

At seven o'clock, seated on the platform as the guest of honour, Ben Chase was served a bad roast beef dinner while various dignitaries talked at him from both sides, breathing over his salad and his half-eaten fruit cup. At eight o'clock the mayor rose to deliver what proved to be a boring panegyric to the city's most famous Vietnam war hero, and half an hour after he had begun, presented Chase with a special scroll detailing his supposed accomplishments and restating the city's pride in him. He was also given the keys to a new Mustang convertible which he had not been expecting, a gift from the Merchants' Association.

By nine-thirty Chase was escorted from the Iron Kettle Restaurant to the parking lot where his new car waited. It was an eight-cylinder job with a complete sports package that included automatic transmission with a floor shift, bucket seats, side mirrors, white-walled tyres – and a wickedly sparkling black paint job that contrasted nicely with the crimson racing stripes over the trunk and hood, red accent lines on both sides. At ten minutes after ten, having posed for newspaper photographs with the mayor and the officers of the Merchants' Association, having expressed his gratitude to everyone present, Chase drove away in his reward.

At twenty minutes past ten he passed through the suburban development known as Ashside, doing slightly more than one hundred miles an hour in a forty-mile-an-hour zone. He crossed the three-lane Galasio Boulevard against the light, turned a corner four blocks on at such a speed that he lost control for a moment and sheared off a traffic sign. At ten-thirty he started up the long slope of Kanackaway Ridge Road, trying to see if he could hold the speed above a hundred clear to the summit. It was a dangerous bit of play, but he did not particularly care if he killed himself.

Perhaps because it had not yet been broken in, or perhaps because the car simply had not been designed for that kind of driving, it would not perform as he wished. Though he held the accelerator to the floor, the speedometer registered at eighty by the time he was two-thirds of the way up the winding road and had fallen to seventy when he crested the rise. He took his foot off the gas pedal, the fire momentarily burned out of him, and let the sleek machine glide along the flat stretch of two-lane that edged the ridge above the city.

Below lay a panorama of lights to stir the hearts of lovers. Though the left side of the road lay against a sheer rock wall, the right was maintained as a park. Fifty yards of grassy verge, dotted with shrubs, led to a restraining rail near the lip of the cliff. Beyond, the sometimes squared and sometimes twisting streets of the city were exposed like an electric map, with special concentrations of light toward the downtown area and out near the gateway Mall shopping centre. Lovers, mostly teenagers, parked here, separated by stands of pine and rows of brambles. An appreciation of the dazzling city turned, in most every case, dozens of times a night, to appreciation of each other.

Once, it had even been that way for Chase.

He pulled the car to the berm, braked and cut the motor. The stillness of the night seemed complete for a moment, deep and noiseless. Then he heard the crickets, a call of an owl somewhere close by, the occasional laughter of young people muffled by closed car windows.

Until he heard that laughter, it did not occur to Chase to wonder why he had come here. He had felt oppressed by the mayor, the Merchants' Association and all the rest of them. He had not really wanted the banquet, and certainly not the car, and he had only gone because there seemed no gracious way to reject them. Confronted with their homespun patriotism and their sugar-glazed vision of the war, he felt burdened down with some indefinable load, smothering. Perhaps it was the past, the realization that he had once shared their parochialism. At any rate, free of them, he had struck for that one place in the city that represented quietude and joy, the much-joked-about lovers' lane atop Kanackaway. But there was no quietude here now, for silence only gave his thoughts a chance to build volume. And the joy? There was none of that, either, for he had no girl with him – and would have been no better off even if he were accompanied.

Along the shadowed length of the park, half a dozen cars were slotted against walls of shrubbery, the moonlight glinting on the bumpers and windows. If he had not known the purpose of this retreat, he would have thought all the vehicles were abandoned. But his knowledge and the trace of mist on the inside of the windows gave everyone away. Now and again a shadow moved inside one of the cars, exaggerated and twisted out of proportion by the steamed glass. That and an occasional rustle of leaves as the wind swept down from the top of the ridge were the only things that moved.

Because of this somewhat breathless quality to the scene, and because he viewed it dispassionately, withdrawn from its purpose, he noticed the other bit of movement immediately. Something dropped from a low point on the rock wall to the left and scurried across the blacktop toward the darkness beneath a huge weeping willow tree a hundred feet in front of Chase's car. Though it was bent and moved with the frantic grace of a frightened animal, it had very clearly been a man.

In Vietnam he had developed what almost amounted to a sixth sense, a perception of imminent danger that was uncanny. That alarm was clanging now.

The one thing that did not belong in a lovers' lane at night was a man alone, on foot. The car was a mobile bed, such a part of the seduction, an extension of the seducer, that there was no modern Casanova successful without one.

It was possible, of course, that the man was engaging in some bird-dogging, spotting parkers for his own amusement and their surprise. Chase had been the victim of that game enough times in his high school years to remember it well. However, it was a pastime usually associated with the mannerless or ugly or immature, those kids who hadn't the opportunity to be *inside* the cars where the real action was. It was not, so far as Chase knew, something adults found pleasure in. And this man, easily six foot, had the bearing of an adult, none of the awkwardness of youth. And, too, bird-dogging was a sport most often played in groups as protection against a beating from one of the surprised lovers. This, Chase was suddenly sure, was something else altogether.

The man came out from beneath the willow, still doubled over and running. He stopped against the edge of a bramble row and looked along it at a three-year-old Chevrolet parked at the end, near the safety railing.

Not sure what was happening or what he should do about it, Chase turned in his seat and worked the cover off the ceiling light in the car. He unscrewed the tiny bulb and dropped it in a pocket of his jacket. When he turned front again, he saw that the man was at the same place, watching the Chevrolet, leaning into the brambles as if unaware of them.

A girl laughed, the sound of her voice clear in the night air. Some of the lovers must have found it too warm for closed windows.

CHASE

The man by the brambles moved again, closing in on the Chevrolet.

Quietly, because the man was no more than a hundred and fifty feet from him, Chase opened the door and got out of the Mustang. He let the door stand open, for he was sure the sound of its closing would alert the intruder. He went around the car and started across the grass, which had recently been mown and was slightly damp and slippery underfoot.

Ahead, a light came on in the Chevrolet, diffused by the steamed windows. Someone shouted, and a young girl screamed. She screamed again.

Chase had been walking, and now he ran as the sounds of a fight burgeoned ahead. When he came up on the Chevrolet, he saw the door on the driver's side was open and the intruder was halfway into the front seat, flailing away at something. Shadows bobbled up and down, dipped and pitched against the frosted glass.

'Hold it there!' Chase shouted, almost directly behind the man now.

The stranger reared back, and as he rose from the car Chase saw the knife. The man held it in his right hand, raised as if to plunge it forward into something. His hand and the weapon were covered in blood.

Chase stepped forward the last few feet, slammed the man against the window post. He slipped his arm around and brought it up beneath the man's neck, drew his head back and forced him out onto the grass.

The girl was still screaming.

The stranger swung his arm down and back, trying to catch Chase's thigh with the point of the blade. He was an amateur. Chase twisted, moving out of the arc

6

of the weapon, simultaneously drawing his arm more tightly across the other's windpipe.

Around them, cars were starting up. Trouble in lovers' lane brought guilt aflowering in every teenage mind nearby. No one wanted to stay to see what the problem was.

'Drop it,' Chase said.

The stranger, though he must have been desperate for breath, stabbed backward and missed again.

Chase, suddenly furious, jerked the man onto his toes and applied the last bit of effort necessary to choke him unconscious. In the same instant, the wet grass betrayed him. His feet slithered, twisted, and he went down with the stranger on top. This time the knife took Chase in the meaty part of his thigh, just below the hip, and it was torn from the other man's hand as Chase bucked up, tossing him aside.

The man rolled and got to his feet. He took a few steps toward Chase, looking for the knife, seemed suddenly to realize the formidable nature of his opponent, turned and ran.

'Stop him!' Chase shouted.

But most of the cars had gone. Those still parked along the cliffside reacted to this last uproar just as their more timid comrades had acted to the first cries: lights flicked on, engines started, tyres squealed as they reached the pavement. In a moment the only cars in lovers' lane were the Chevrolet and Chase's Mustang.

The pain in his leg was bad, though not any worse than a hundred others he had endured. In the light from the Chevrolet, he could see that the bleeding was slow, not ugly and rhythmic like the spurt from a torn artery. When he tried, he could stand and walk with little trouble.

He went to the car and looked in, then wished he had not. The body of a young man, perhaps nineteen or twenty, was sprawled half on the seat and half on the floor. In the generous splashes of blood that covered him, streaming from what looked like two dozen knife wounds, there was proof that he could not be alive. Beyond him, curled in the corner by the far door, a petite brunette, a year or two younger than her lover, was moaning softly, her hands gripped so tightly on her knees that they looked more like claws latched about a piece of game. She was wearing a pink miniskirt but no blouse or bra. Her small breasts were spotted with blood, and the nipples were erect.

Chase wondered why he noticed this last detail more plainly than anything else about the grisly scene.

'Stay there,' Chase said. 'I'll come around for you.'

She did not respond, though she continued to moan.

Chase almost closed the door on the driver's side, then realized that he would thereby shut off the light and let the brunette alone in the car with the corpse. He walked around the car, leaning on it so that he could favour his right leg, and opened her door. Apparently these kids had not believed in locks. That was, he supposed, part of their generation's optimism, part and parcel with their theories on free love, mutual trust and brotherhood. It was the same generation that was supposed to live life so fully that they all but denied the existence of death. The expression on the brunette's face, however, indicated that she was no longer trying to deny anything.

'Where's your blouse?' Chase asked.

She was no longer looking at the corpse, but she was not looking at him either. She stared at her knees, at her whitened knuckles, and she mumbled.

Chase groped around on the floor under her legs and found the balled-up garment. 'You better put this on,' he said.

She would not take it from him. She continued to mumble.

'Come on, now,' he said as gently as he could. He was perfectly aware that the killer might not have gone very far.

She seemed to be saying something, though her voice was lower than before. When he bent closer to listen, he discovered that she was saying, 'Please don't hurt me. Please don't.'

'I'm not going to hurt you,' Chase said, straightening up. 'I didn't do that to your boyfriend. But the man who did might still be hanging around. My car's up along the road. Will you please come with me?'

She looked up at him then, blinked, shook her head and got out of the car. He handed her the blouse, which she unrolled and shook out but could not seem to get on. She was still in a state of shock

'You can put it on in my car,' Chase said. 'It's safer there.' All around, the shadows under the trees seemed deeper than before.

He put his arm around her and half carried her back to the Mustang. The door on the passenger's side was locked. By the time he got her around and through the other door and had followed her inside, she seemed to have recovered some of her senses. She slipped one arm in the blouse, then the other, and slowly buttoned it. Apparently she had not been wearing a bra. When he closed and locked his door and started the engine, she said, 'Who are you?'

'Passer-by,' he said, 'I saw the fellow and thought something was wrong.'

'He killed Mike,' she said.

'Your boyfriend?'

She did not respond to that but leaned back against the seat, chewing her lip and wiping absent-mindedly at the few spots of blood on her face.

Chase swung the car around and started down Kanackaway Ridge Road at the same pace he had come up, took the turn at the bottom so fast that she was thrown painfully against the door.

'Buckle your seatbelt,' he said.

She did as he directed, but she appeared to be in the same unresponsive mood, staring straight ahead at the steets that unrolled before them.

'Who was he?' Chase asked as they reached the intersection at Galasio Boulevard and took it with the light this time.

'Mike,' she said.

'Not your boyfriend. The other one.'

'I don't know,' she said.

'Did you see his face?'

She nodded.

'You didn't recognize him?'

'No.'

'I thought it might be an old lover, a rejected suitor, something like that.'

She said nothing.

Her reluctance to talk about it gave Chase time to consider the affair. He began to wonder, as he recalled the killer's approach from the top of the ridge, whether the man had known which car he was after or whether any car would have done, whether this had been an act of revenge directed against Mike specifically or if it was only the work of a madman. The papers, even before he had been sent overseas, had been filled with stories of meaningless slaughter. He had not read any papers since his discharge, but he suspected the same brand of senselessness still flourished. That possibility made him uncomfortable. It was so similar to Nam, to Operation Jules Verne and his part in it, that very bad old memories were stirred . . .

Fifteen minutes after they left the ridge top, Chase parked in front of police headquarters on Kensington Avenue.

'Are you feeling well enough to talk with them?' Chase asked.

'The police?'

'Yes.'

She shrugged. 'I guess so.' She had recovered remarkably fast. She even thought, now, to take Chase's pocket comb and run it through her dark hair several times. 'How do I look?'

'Fine,' he said, wondering if it were not better to go without a woman than to leave behind one who grieved so brief a time as this.

'Let's go,' she said. She opened her door and stepped out, her lovely, trim legs flashing in a rustle of brief cloth.

The door of the small grey room opened, admitting an equally small and grey man. His face was lined, his

11

eyes sunken as if he had not had any sleep in a day or two. His light brown hair was uncombed and in need of a trim. He crossed to the table behind which Chase and the girl sat, took the only chair left and folded into it as if he would never get up again. He said, 'I'm Detective Wallace.'

'Glad to meet you,' Chase said, though he was not glad at all.

The girl was quiet, looking at her nails.

'Now, what's this all about?' Wallace asked, folding his hands on the top of the scarred table and looking at each of them, much like a priest or counsellor.

'I already told the desk sergeant most of it,' Chase said.

'He isn't in homicide. I am,' Wallace said. 'Who was murdered and how?'

Chase said, 'Her boyfriend, stabbed.'

'Can't she speak?'

'I can speak,' the girl said.

'What's your name?'

'Louise.'

'Louise what?'

'Allenby. Louise Allenby,' she said.

Wallace said, 'You live in the city?'

'In Ashside.'

'How old?'

She looked at him as if she would flare up, then turned her gaze back at her nails again. 'Seventeen.'

'In high school?'

'I graduated in June,' she said. 'I'm going to college in the fall, to Penn State.'

Wallace said. 'Who was the boy?'

'Mike. Michael Karnes.'

'Just a boyfriend, or you engaged?'

'Boyfriend,' she said. 'We'd been going together for about a year, kind of steady.'

'What were you doing on Kanackaway Ridge Road?' Wallace asked.

She looked at him, levelly this time. 'What do you think?'

'Look,' Chase interjected, 'is this really necessary? The girl wasn't involved in it. I think the man with the knife might have tried for her next if I – hadn't stopped him.'

Wallace turned more toward Chase. He said, 'How'd you happen to be there in the first place?'

'Just out driving,' Chase said.

Wallace looked at him a long moment, then said, 'What's your name?'

'Benjamin Chase.'

'I *thought* I'd seen you before,' the detective said. His manner softened immediately. 'Your picture was in the papers today.'

Chase nodded.

'That was really something you did over there,' Wallace said. 'That really took guts.'

'It wasn't as much as they make out,' Chase said.

'I'll bet it wasn't!' Wallace said, though it was clear that he thought it must even have been more than the papers had made it. He turned to the girl, who had taken a new interest in Chase, studying him from the corners of her eyes. His tone toward her had changed too. He said, 'You want to tell me about it, just how it happened?'

She did, losing some of her composure in the process. Twice Chase thought that she was going to cry, and he wished that she would have. Her cold manner, so soon afterward, made him uneasy. Maybe she *was* still trying to deny the existence of death. She held the tears back, and by the time she had finished she was herself again.

'You saw his face?' Wallace asked.

'Yes.'

'Can you describe him?'

'Not really,' she said. 'He had brown eyes, I think.'

'No moustache or beard?'

'I don't think so.'

'Long sideburns or short?'

'Short, I think.'

'Any scars?'

'No.'

'Anything at all memorable about him, the shape of his face, whether his hair was receding or full, anything?'

'I can't remember,' she said.

Chase said, 'When I got to her, she was in a state of shock. I doubt that she was seeing anything and registering it properly.'

Instead of a grateful agreement, Louise turned an angry look at him. He remembered, too late, that the worst thing for someone Louise's age was to lose your cool, to fail to cope. He had betrayed her momentary lapse to, of all people, a policeman. She would have little gratitude for him now, whether or not he saved her life.

Wallace got up. 'Come on,' he said.

'Where?' Chase asked.

'We'll go out there, with some of the lab boys.'

'Is that really necessary?' Chase asked.

14

'Well, I have to take statements from you, both of you, in more detail than this. It would help, Mr Chase, to be on the scene when you're describing it again.' He smiled, as if again impressed with Chase's identity, and said, 'It'll only take a short while. We'll need the girl longer than we will you.'

Chase was sitting in the rear of Wallace's squad car, thirty feet from the scene of the murder, answering questions, when the staff car from the *Press-Dispatch* arrived. Two photographers and a reporter got out. For the first time Chase realized what they were going to do with the story. They were going to make him a hero. Again.

'Please,' he said to Wallace, 'can we keep the reporters from knowing who helped the girl?'

'Why?'

'I'm tired of reporters,' Chase said.

Wallace said, 'But you did save her life. You ought to be proud of that.'

'I don't want to talk to them,' Chase said.

'That's up to you,' Wallace said. 'But I'm afraid they'll have to know who interrupted the killer. It'll be in the report, and the report is open to the press.'

Later, when Wallace was finished with him and he was getting out of the car to join another officer who would take him back to town, the girl put a hand on his shoulder. 'Thank you,' she said.

At the same instant a photographer snapped a picture, the flashbulb spraying light that lasted for what seemed an eternity.

In the car, on the way back to town, the uniformed officer behind the wheel said his name was Don Jones,

15

that he had read about Chase and that he would like to have Chase's autograph for his kids. Chase signed his name on the back of a homicide report blank, and at Jones's urging, prefaced it with 'To Rick and Judy Jones.' The officer asked a lot of questions about Nam which Chase answered as shortly as courtesy would allow.

In his Mustang, he drove more sedately than he had before. There was no anger in him now, nothing but an infinite weariness.

At a quarter past one in the morning he parked in front of Mrs Fiedling's house, relieved that there were no lights burning. He unlocked the front door as quietly as the ancient lock would permit, stepped knowingly around most of the loose boards in the staircase, and finally made his way to his attic apartment – one large room which served as a kitchen, bedroom and living room, a walk-in closet and a private bath. He locked his door. He felt safe now. He did not have to talk to Mrs Fiedling or, against his will, look down her perpetually unbuttoned housedress at the fish-belly curves of her sagging and altogether unerotic breasts, wondering why she had to be so casually immodest at her age.

He undressed, washed his face and hands, studied the knife wound in his thigh, which he had neglected to mention to the police. It was shallow, already clotted and beginning to dry into a thin scab. He washed it, flushed it with alcohol, swabbed Merthiolate over it. In the main room, he completed the medication by pouring a glass of Jack Daniel's over two ice cubes, and sank down on the bed with the wonderful stuff. He usually consumed a fifth of it a day. Today, because of that damned banquet, he had been forced to stay off it. Drinking, he felt clean again. Alone with a bottle of good liquor was the only time he felt clean.

He was pouring his second glassful over the same half-melted ice cubes when the telephone rang.

When he first moved into the apartment, he had protested that he did not require a telephone, since no one would be calling him and since he had no wish to contact anyone else. Mrs Fiedling had not believed him, and envisioning a situation wherein she would become a messenger service for him, insisted on a telephone hook-up as a condition of occupancy.

That was long before she knew that he was a hero. It was even before *he* knew it.

For months the phone went unused, except when she called up from downstairs to tell him mail had been delivered or to invite him to dinner. Since the announcement by the White House, however, since all the excitement about the medal, he received two and three calls a day, most of them from perfect strangers who offered congratulations he did not want or sought interviews for various publications he had never read. He cut most of them short. Thus far, no one had gall enough to ring him up this late at night, but he supposed he could never regain the solitude he had grown used to in those first months after his discharge.

He considered ignoring the phone, concentrating on his Jack Daniel's until it had stopped crying. But when it had rung for the sixteenth time, he realized the caller was a good bit more persistent than he, and he answered it. 'Hello?'

'Chase?'

'Yes.'

'Do you know me?'

'No,' he said, unable to place the voice. The man sounded tired – but aside from that one clue, he might have been anywhere between twenty and sixty years old, fat or thin, tall or short.

'How's your leg, Chase?' His voice contained a hint of humour, though the reason for it escaped Chase.

'Good enough,' Chase said. 'Fine.'

'You're very good with your hands.'

Chase said nothing, could not bring himself to speak, for he had begun to understand just what the call was all about.

'Very good with your hands,' the stranger repeated. 'I guess you learned that in the army.'

'Yes,' Chase said.

'I guess you learned a lot of things in the army, and I guess you think you can take care of yourself pretty well.'

Chase said, 'Is this *you*?'

The man laughed, momentarily shaking off the dull tone of exhaustion. 'Yes, it's me,' he said. 'I've got a badly bruised throat, and I know my voice will be just awful by morning. Otherwise, I got away about as lightly as you did, Chase.'

Chase remembered, with a clarity his mind reserved for moments of danger, the struggle with the killer on the grass by the Chevrolet. He tried to get a clear picture of the man's face but could not do any better for his own sake than for the police. He said, 'How did you know that I was the one who stopped you?'

18

CHASE

'I saw your picture in the paper,' the man said. 'You're a war hero. Your picture was everywhere. When you were lying on your back, beside the knife, I recognized you and got out of there fast.'

Chase said, 'Who are you?'

'Do you really expect me to say?' There was a definite note of amusement in the man's voice.

Chase had forgotten his drink altogether. The alarms, the goddamned alarms in his head, were ringing at peak volume. It might have been a national holiday, judging by that mental clangor. Chase said. 'What do you want?'

The stranger was silent for so long that Chase almost asked the same question again. Suddenly, the amusement gone from his voice, the killer said, 'You messed in where you had no right messing. You don't know the trouble I went to, picking the proper targets out of all those young fornicators, the ones who most deserved to die. I planned it for weeks, Chase, and I had given that young sinner his deserved punishment. The young woman was left, and you saved her before I could perform my duty, saved a whore like that who had no right to be spared.'

'You're not well,' Chase said. He realized the absurdity of that statement the moment he had spoken, but the killer had reduced him to clichés.

'I just wanted to tell you, Mr Chase, that it doesn't end here, not by a long shot.' The killer either did not hear or pretended not to hear what Chase had said.

'What do you mean?'

'I'll deal with you, Chase, once I've researched your background and have weighed a proper judgment on you. Then, when you've been made to pay, I'll deal with the whore, that girl.'

'Deal with?' Chase asked. The euphemism reminded him of all the similar evasions of vocabulary he had grown accustomed to in Nam. He felt much older than he was, more tired than he had a moment earlier.

'I'm going to kill you, Chase. I'm going to punish you for whatever sins are on your record, and because you've messed in where you had no right.' He waited a moment. 'Do you understand?'

'Yes, but –'

'I'll be talking to you again, Chase.'

'Look, if –'

The man hung up.

Chase put his own receiver in the cradle of the phone and leaned back against the headboard of the bed. He felt something cold and awkward in his hand, looked down and was surprised to find the glass of whiskey. He raised it to his lips and took a taste. It was slightly bitter.

He had to decide what to do about the call.

The police would be interested, of course, for they would see it as their first solid lead to the man who had killed Michael Karnes. They would probably want to monitor the line in hopes the man would call again – especially since he had said that Chase would be hearing from him again. They might even station an officer in Chase's room, and they were certain to put a tail on him both for his own protection and for a chance to nab the murderer if he should try for a second victim. Yet . . .

The last few weeks, since the news about the Medal of Honor, Chase's day-to-day routines had been utterly destroyed. He had been accustomed to a deep solitude, disturbed only by his need to talk to store clerks and to Mrs Fiedling, his landlady. In the mornings he went downtown and had breakfast at Woolworth's. He bought a paperback, occasionally a magazine – but never a newspaper – picked up what incidentals he required, stopped twice a week at the liquor store, spent the noon hour in the park watching the girls in their short skirts as they walked to and from their jobs, then went home and spent the rest of the day in his room. He read during the long afternoons, and he drank. By evening he could not clearly see the print on the pages, and he turned on the small television set to watch the old movies he had almost memorized detail by detail. Around eleven o'clock at night he finished the day's bottle, having eaten little or nothing for supper, and then he slept.

It was not much, he supposed, certainly not what he had once thought would constitute a reasonable life style, but it was bearable. Because it was simple, it was also solid, easy to work within, empty of doubt and uncertainty, lacking in choices and decisions that might bring about another breakdown. Then, when the AP and UPI carried the story of the Vietnam hero who had declined to personally attend a White House ceremony for the awarding of the Congressional Medal of Honor (though he had not declined the medal itself, since he felt that would bring more publicity than he could handle), there was no time or opportunity for simplicity.

He had weathered the uproar, the sentiment and enthusiasm, somehow, granting as few interviews as possible, talking in monosyllables on the phone. The only thing for which he was forced to leave his room was the banquet, and he had been able to cope with that only because he knew that once it was over, he could return to his attic apartment and pick up the uneventful life that had so recently been wrenched away from him.

The incident in lovers' lane had changed his plans, postponed a return to stability. The papers would carry it again, front page and with pictures. There would be more calls, more congratulations, more interviewers to be turned down. Then it would die out, in a week or two – if he could tolerate it that long – and things would be as they had once been, quiet and manageable.

He took another sip of his drink. It tasted better than it had a short while ago.

There were limits to what he could endure, however. Two more weeks of newspaper stories, telephone calls, job offers and marriage proposals would take him to the end of his meagre resources. If, during that same time, he had to share his room with an officer of the law and be followed everywhere he went, he would not hold up. Already he felt the same vague emptiness filling him that had filled him so completely in the hospital. It was that lack of purpose, that loss of desire to go on that he must stave off at all costs. Even if it meant withholding information from the authorities.

He wouldn't tell the police about the call.

He took more of his drink, went to the cupboard and refreshed it with another slug from the dark bottle.

After all, it was unlikely that the killer was serious.

CHASE

He had to be a madman, for no sane person would attack a couple in a parked car and hack one of them nearly to pieces with a long-bladed butcher knife. Madmen were dangerous, to be sure, but they rarely ever did what they promised to do. Or, at least, that was what Chase thought.

He understood that he was keeping a lead from the police, a contact they might make good use of. But the police were clever. They would find the man without Chase's aid. They must have fingerprints from the door handle of the Chevrolet, from the handle of the murder weapon. They had already thought to issue a statement that the killer would be suffering from a badly bruised throat and the resultant laryngitis. What he was keeping from them would do little to speed up their efficient system of detection and apprehension.

He finished his drink. It had gone down quickly, smoothly.

It was decided.

He poured more whiskey and went back to bed, slid beneath the covers and stared at the blank eye of the television set. In a few days everything would be back to normal. He could settle into old routines, living comfortably on his disability pension and the moderately ample inheritance from his parents' estate. There would be no need to get a job or to talk to anyone or to make decisions. His only task would be to consume enough whiskey to be able to sleep despite the nightmares.

He finished his glassful. He slept.

Two

Chase rose early the next morning, frightened awake by nightmares full of dead men who were trying to talk to him. After that, the day deteriorated.

His mistake was in trying to go on with it in a manner that denied anything unusual had happened. He rose, bathed, shaved, dressed and went downstairs to see if there was any mail on the hall table for him. There was none, but Mrs Fiedling heard him and hurried out of the perpetually darkened living room to show him the first edition of the *Press-Dispatch*. His picture was on the front page, turned half toward Louise Allenby getting out of the squad car. She looked as if she was crying, one hand gripping his arm, far more full of grief than she had actually been.

'I'm so proud of you,' Mrs Fiedling said. She sounded like his mother. Indeed, she was old enough for the post, in her mid-fifties. Her hair was curled tightly in an old-fashioned style and shot through with grey. Her doughy face had been rouged and lipsticked and had, peculiarly, been made to look ten years older by those cosmetic tricks. She was twenty or thirty pounds too heavy and carried nearly all of it in her hips.

'It wasn't anything like they said, not as exciting as that,' Chase told her.

'How do you know? You haven't read it.'

'They always overwrite. I know, because they did it the last time.'

'Oh, you're just too modest,' Mrs Fiedling said. She was wearing a blue and yellow housedress with the two top buttons opened. He could see not only the pallid bulge of her breasts, but the edge of a yellowed brassiere as well.

Though he was much larger and much younger than Mrs Fiedling, with three times her strength, she frightened him. It was, he had once decided, because he did not know what she wanted from him.

She said, 'I bet this brings twice the job offers that the last article brought!'

Mrs Fiedling was much more interested in Chase's eventual employment than was Chase himself. At first he had thought that she was afraid he would fall in arrears on the rent, but he eventually decided that she believed him about his inheritance and that her concern went deeper than that.

She said, 'As I've often told you, you're young and strong, and you have a lifetime ahead of you. The thing for a fellow like you is work, hard work, a chance to make something of yourself. Not that you haven't done all right so far. But this lounging around, not working – it hasn't been good for you. You must have lost fifteen pounds since you first moved in.'

Chase did not respond.

Mrs Fiedling moved closer to him and took the morning paper out of his hands. She looked at the picture in the centre of the front page and sighed.

'I have to be going,' Chase said.

She looked up from the paper. 'I *saw* your car.'

'Yes,' he said.

'It tells about it in the paper. Wasn't that nice of them, though?'

'Yes.'

'They hardly ever do anything for the boys who serve and don't make a big protest of it. You read all about the bad ones, but no one lifts a hand for good boys like you. It's about time, and I hope you enjoy the car.'

'I will,' he said, opening the front door and stepping outside before she could carry on any further.

The nightmare, Mrs Fiedling, then breakfast, one bit of bad business after the other . . .

Ordinarily, the counter at Woolworth's was a guarantee of privacy, even if every stool was taken. Businessmen reading the financial pages, secretaries drinking coffee and chattering each other fully awake, labourers slumped forward over greasy eggs and potatoes that their wives had not risen to fix for them – none of the customers wanted to talk or be noticed. The proximity of the seats, the elbow-to-elbow circumstances left no room for graceful dining unless one could pretend that there was really no one else about. That Tuesday morning, however, Chase discovered, halfway through his meal, that most of the other people there were watching him with only poorly disguised interest.

When he had sat down, the pert little blonde waitress had said, 'Good morning, Mr Chase. What will you have?' He should have known then that everything was not as it should be, for he had never been on friendly terms with her and had never told her his name. The ubiquitous newspaper, spread across with his likeness, betrayed him wherever he went.

He stopped eating halfway through, left a tip, paid his bill and got out of there. His hands were shaking, and the backs of his knees quivered as if his legs would let him down.

He went to the newsstand to purchase a paperback and was confronted with so many copies of his own face in the paper racks that he turned away at the door without going in.

At the liquor store, the clerk commented on the size of his purchase for the first time in months. Clearly, he seemed to feel it was improper for a man like Chase to drink so much. Unless, of course, the whiskey was for a party. He asked Chase if he was giving a party. Chase said that he was.

Then, anxious for the barren confines of his little attic room, he walked two blocks toward home before he remembered that he now had a car. He walked back to it, embarrassed that someone might have seen his confusion, and when he settled in behind the wheel he felt too tightly wound to risk driving. He sat there for fifteen minutes, looking through the service manual, the ownership papers and the temporary owner's card, then started the engine and drove home.

CHASE

He did not go to the park to watch the girls on their lunch hour, because he feared recognition. If one of them should come over to him and try to strike up a conversation, he would not know what to do.

In his room, he poured a glass of whiskey over two ice cubes and stirred it with his finger.

He turned on the television and found an old movie starring Wallace Beery and Marie Dressler. He had seen it at least half a dozen times, but he kept it on just the same. The repetition, the stability of the sequential scenes – through thousands of showings in movies theatres and on television – soothed his nerves. He watched Wallace Beery make a clumsy romantic pass at Marie Dressler, and the familiarity of that awkwardness, seen so often before and in that same exact detail, was like a balm on his mind.

At 11:05 the telephone rang.

He finally answered it, denied permission for an interview and hung up.

At 11:26 it rang again.

This time it was the insurance agent with whom the Merchants' Association had taken out a year's policy on the Mustang, in Chase's name. He wanted to know if the coverage was adequate or whether Chase would like to increase it for a nominal sum. He was upset when Chase said it was adequate.

At 11:50 the phone rang a third time. When Chase picked it up, the killer said, 'Hello, how has your morning been?'

Chase said, 'What do you want?'

'Did you see the papers?' His voice was hoarse, a loud whisper.

'One of them.'

28

'Lovely coverage of your heroism, a great deal of purple prose, don't you think?'

'I don't like publicity,' Chase said, hoping to put himself in the man's good graces, even while he understood their roles should be reversed.

'You have a knack for getting it, all the same.'

'What do you want?' Chase repeated.

'To tell you to be by your phone at six this evening. I have spent the morning researching your biography, and I have similar plans for the afternoon. At six I'll tell you what I've found.'

Chase said, 'What's the purpose in that?'

'I can't very well pass judgment on you until I know what sort of transgressions you're guilty of, can I?' Under the pervading wheeze of protesting vocal cords lay a trace of that amusement Chase had previously noticed. The man said, 'You see, I didn't randomly select which fornicators I would punish up on Kanackaway.'

'You didn't?'

'No, I researched the situation.' The man chuckled, an indulgence that strained his damaged throat and made him cough like a heavy smoker. When he had control of his voice again, he said, 'I went up there every night for two weeks and copied licence-plate numbers. Then I matched them up until I found the one most often repeated.'

Chase said, 'Why?'

'To discover the most deserving sinners,' the stranger said. 'In this state, for two dollars, the Bureau of Motor Vehicles will trace a licence number for you. I had that done and learned the identity of the boy who owned the car. From there, it was a simple matter to investigate his background and to learn the name of his partner in these activities. She was the third girl that he had gone with, steadily, and she was not the only one he entertained on Kanackaway even when she thought he saw her and no one else. She had her own promiscuous affairs, too. I followed her, twice, when other boys picked her up, and one of those times she gave herself to her date.'

'How do you know all this?' Chase asked.

'Listen to me,' the stranger said. 'Never mind my methods.' His anger sent him into another coughing fit. When he was recovered, he said, 'They were both sluts, the boy as well as the girl. They deserved exactly what they were to have gotten – except that you saved her.'

Chase waited.

The man said, 'You see, I must research you as thoroughly as I did those first two. Otherwise, I would never be sure if you deserved the judgment of death or whether I had murdered you simply because you had interfered with my plans and I wanted revenge. In short, I am not killing people. I am executing those who deserve it.'

Chase said, 'I don't want you calling here again.'

'You can stop me?'

'I'll have the line bugged.'

'That won't stop me,' the stranger said, again amused. 'I'll simply place the calls from various booths around the city, and I'll keep them too short to trace.'

'If I refuse to answer my phone?' Chase asked.

'You'll answer it.'

'What makes you sure?'

CHASE

'You'll want to know what I've learned about you, and you'll want to know when I've passed judgment on you, when you'll die.' His voice had grown progressively less audible through the last dozen words, and now he seemed unwilling to force it any longer. 'Six o'clock this evening,' he reminded Chase, then hung up.

Chase dropped the receiver, uneasily aware that the killer knew him better than he knew himself. He would answer every time, of course. And for the same reasons he had answered all the nuisance calls of the last few weeks rather than obtain an unlisted number. The only problem was that he did not know just what those reasons were.

Impulsively, he lifted the receiver and placed a call to the police headquarters downtown. It was the first time in ten and a half months that he had used the dial, initiated a call. The police number, along with the numbers of the firehouse and River Rescue, was on a sticker at the base of the phone, as if someone had wanted to make it as easy as possible for him to make this move.

When the desk sergeant answered, Chase asked for Wallace, gave his name. At the moment he was not above using his present fame to cut red tape.

'Yes, Mr Chase, can I help?' Wallace asked.

He did not say what he had intended to. Instead he asked, 'How is the investigation coming along?'

Wallace was not averse to talking shop. 'Slowly but surely,' he told Chase. 'We found prints on the knife and sent copies of them into Washington and to the state capital. If he's ever been arrested for a serious crime or if he's worked for any branch of the

31

government, we'll have him in twenty-four hours.'

'And if he's never been printed?'

Wallace said, 'We'll get him anyway. We found a man's ring in the Chevy. It didn't belong to the dead boy, and it looks as if it would be too small for your fingers by a size or three. Didn't lose a ring, did you?'

'No,' Chase said.

'I thought so. Should have called you on it, but I was pretty sure about it. It's his, right enough.'

'Anything else besides the prints and ring?'

'We're keeping a constant watch on the girl and her parents, though I'd appreciate it if you didn't say anything about that to anyone. We'd like to see him try for her where we could get at him.'

'Might he?'

'If he thinks she can identify him, yes. Remember, he knows she got a good long look at his face, and he has no way of knowing how badly her mind was working then.'

'I guess so.'

'It's occurred to me that we wouldn't be far off if we gave you a tail as well. Have you thought of that?'

Alarmed out of proportion by the suggestion, Chase said, 'No. I don't see what value that would have.'

'Well,' Wallace observed, 'the story was in the papers this morning. Though he probably doesn't fear you identifying him as much as the girl, he might bear a grudge of some sort.'

'He'd have to be a madman, then.'

'What else is he, Mr Chase?'

'You mean you've found no motives from questioning the girl, no old lovers who might have –'

'No,' Wallace said. 'Right now we're operating on the assumption that there was no rational motive, that we're dealing with a psychotic.'

'I see.'

'Well,' Wallace said, 'I'm sorry there isn't more solid news.'

'And I'm sorry to have bothered you,' Chase said. 'You've probably not had much sleep.'

'None,' Wallace admitted.

They said goodbye, and Chase hung up without telling him a thing, though he had intended to spill it all. A twenty-four-hour guard on the girl. They would do the same to him, worse if they knew he'd been contacted. The walls seemed to sway, alternately closing in like the jaws of an immense vice and swinging out like flat grey gates. The floor rose and fell like waves. Instability swelled around him, the very thing that had landed him in the hospital and had eventually led to his seventy-five-percent disability pension. He could not let it take hold again, and he knew the best way to fight it was to constrict the perimeters of his world, gain solace from solitude. He went to get another drink.

The telephone woke him from his nap just as the dead men, standing in a ring around him, reached for him with soft, white, corrupted hands. He sat straight up in bed and cried out, his arms held before him to ward off their cold touch. When he saw where he was and that he was alone, he sank back, exhausted, and listened to the ringing. Insistently, the thing sounded again and again until, after thirty harsh explosions, he had no choice but to pick it up.

'Yes.'

'I was about to come check on you,' Mrs Fiedling said. 'Are you all right?'

'I'm okay' he said.

'It took you so long to answer.'

'I was asleep.'

She hesitated, as if framing what she was about to say. 'I'm having Swiss steak, mushrooms, baked corn and mashed potatoes for supper. Would you like to come down; there's more than I can use.'

'I don't think –'

'A strapping boy like you needs his regular meals,' she said.

'I've already eaten.'

She was silent for a long while, then said, 'All right. But I wish you'd waited, 'cause I got all this food.'

'I'm sorry, but I'm stuffed,' he said.

'Tomorrow night, maybe.'

'Maybe,' he said. He rang off before she could suggest a late-night snack together.

The ice melted in his glass, diluting what whiskey he had not drunk. He emptied the sadly coloured result into the bathroom sink, got new ice and a new shot of liquor. It tasted as bitter as a bite of lemon rind. He drank it anyway. There was nothing else in the cupboard or refrigerator but a bag of Winesap apples, and they would be infinitely worse.

He turned on the small black-and-white television set again and rotated the dial slowly through all the local channels, found nothing but the news and a single cartoon programme. He watched the cartoons.

None of them were funny.

After that was over, he found an old movie and let

the dial set on it.

The stack of glasses on the cupboard left no room for him to place his present glass when he was finished with it. He carried them into the bathroom and washed them in the sink with hot water and Ivory soap, dried them with a clean towel and returned them to the cupboard.

Except for the phone call, he had the whole evening ahead of him.

At six o'clock on the nose, the telephone rang.

'Hello?'

'Good evening, Chase,' the killer said. His voice was still awful.

Chase sat down on the bed.

'How are you tonight?'

'Okay,' Chase said.

'You know what I've been up to all day?'

'Research.'

'That's right.'

'Tell me what you found,' Chase said, as if all of it would be news to him even though he was the subject. And maybe it *would* be.

'First of all, you were born here a little over twenty-four years ago on June 11, 1947, in Mercy Hospital. Your parents died in an automobile accident when you were eighteen. You went to school at State and graduated in a three-year accelerated programme, having majored in business administration. You did well in all subjects except a few required courses, chiefly Basic Physical Sciences, Biology I and II, Chemistry I and Basic Composition.' The killer whispered on for three more long minutes, listing impersonal facts that Chase had thought ended with himself. But courthouse records, college files, newspaper morgues and half a dozen other sources had provided far more information about his life than the killer could have gleaned from the recent articles in the *Press-Dispatch*.

'I think I've been on the line about five minutes,' the killer said. 'It's time I went to another booth. Is your phone tapped, Chase?'

'No,' Chase said.

'Just the same, I'll hang up now and call you back in a few minutes.' The line went dead, hissing in Chase's ear like a snake.

Five minutes later the killer called again.

'What I gave you before was just so much dry grass, Chase. But let me add a few more things and do some speculating; let's see if I can add a match to that dry grass.'

'What do you mean?' Chase asked.

'For one thing,' the man said, 'you inherited a lot of money, but you haven't spent much of it. Thirty thousand after taxes, but you live frugally.'

'How would you know that?'

'I drove by your house today and discovered you live in a furnished apartment on the third floor. When I saw you coming home, it was apparent that you don't sink much into a nice wardrobe. Until you won your Mustang through bravery, you didn't have a car. It follows, then, that you must have a great deal of your inheritance left, what with the monthly disability pension from the government to pay most or all of your bills.'

'I want you to stop checking on me,' Chase said hotly. He was suddenly more terrified of this stranger than of all the dead men in his nightmares. He was beginning to feel like a subject on exhibition, housed in a glass cage, all the faces in the world pressed against the walls, peering in.

The man laughed. 'I can hardly stop. Remember the necessity to evaluate your moral content before passing judgment, Mr Chase.'

Chase hung up this time. The fact that he had taken the initiative cheered him considerably. When it began to ring again, he summoned up the will not to answer it. After thirty rings, it stopped. When it rang again, ten minutes later, however, he picked it up and said hello.

The killer was furious, straining his ruined throat to the limit. 'If you ever do that again, you rotten son of a bitch, you'll be sorry! It won't be a clean kill. I'll see to that. Do you understand me?'

'Yes,' Chase said, feeling ill.

The stranger calmed at once. 'Something else, Mr Chase. That "wounded in action" bit excites me. You don't appear disabled enough to deserve a pension, and you more than held your own in our fight. That gives me ideas. It makes me think your wounds aren't physical at all.'

Chase said, 'Oh?' His heart was beating too fast and his mouth had gone dry.

'I think you had psychological problems that put you in that army hospital and got you a discharge.' He waited.

'You're wrong,' Chase said.

'Maybe, maybe not. I'll have to take more time to check into it, that's all. Well, rest easy tonight, Mr Chase. You're not scheduled to die yet.'

CHASE

'Wait!' Chase said.

'Yes?'

'I have to have a name for you. I can't go on thinking of you in totally abstract terms like "the man" and "the stranger" and "the killer." Do you see how that is?'

'Yes,' the man admitted.

'A name?'

He considered a moment, then said, 'You can call me Judge.'

'Judge?'

'Yes, as in "Judge, jury and executioner," Mr Chase.' He laughed until he coughed, then hung up, like a prankster.

Chase went to the refrigerator and got an apple. He carried it to the table and put it down on a napkin, went to get a paring knife from the utilities drawer. He peeled the apple and cut it into eight sections, chewing each one thoroughly. He supposed it was not much of a supper, but then there were a lot of energy-giving calories in a glass of whiskey. He poured himself a few ounces over ice, for dessert.

He washed his hands, which had become sticky with apple juice.

With another drink, he went to the bed and sat down, staring through the movie on the television screen. He tried not to think about anything except the routines he was used to, the things he relied on. Breakfast at Woolworth's, paperback reading material, liquor purchases. Old movies on television, the twenty-eight thousand dollars in the savings account, his pension cheque, the wonderful bottle a day. Those things were what counted, what gave life

CHASE

its substance. Anything else was misleading, dross
that had no place in his scheme of things.
Again he refrained from calling the police.

Three

The nightmares were so bad that Chase slept fitfully, waking repeatedly at the penultimate moment of horror, redreaming the tight circle of dead men and the silent harangue that they directed against him as they closed in with their hands outstretched . . .

He rose early, abandoning any hope of rest, bathed and shaved, sat down at the table and peeled an apple for breakfast. He did not want to face the regular customers at Woolworth's counter now that he was something more than just another face to them, yet he could not think of another place where he could go unrecognized. The apple was not much on which to start the day. He decided that he would have to go out for lunch if he could remember the name of a restaurant where one could have some degree of privacy.

After lunch, of course, he could survive on Jack Daniel's quite nicely.

CHASE

The time was 9:35 in the morning.

It was much too early to begin drinking, for he would only make himself ill hitting a bottle already. After lunch. But what could he do with the long hours between now and noon? He turned on the television but couldn't find any old movies, turned it off. He had read what books there were in the room.

At last, with nothing to do, he began to recall the details of the nightmare that had wakened him, and he knew that was no good. He picked up the phone; for the second time he placed a call, working the unfamiliar dial clumsily.

It rang three times before a pert young woman answered. She said. 'Dr Cauvel's office, Miss Pringle speaking, can I help you?'

Chase said, 'I'd like to see the doctor.'

'Are you a regular patient?'

'Yes. My name's Ben Chase.'

'Oh, yes!' Miss Pringle said, as if it were a small joy to be hearing from him. 'Good morning, Mr Chase.' She rattled the pages of an appointment book and said. 'Your regularly scheduled visit is this Friday afternoon at three.'

'I have to see Dr Cauvel before that,' Chase said. When he first conceived of this irregular contact, he had not been at all sure if it was wise. Now it seemed not only wise, but wildly important. 'I *must* see him.'

'Tomorrow morning we have half an hour –'

Chase interrupted her. 'Today.'

'I beg your pardon?' Miss Pringle said, her joy at hearing his voice having diminished appreciably.

'I want an appointment today,' Chase repeated.

Miss Pringle attempted to inform him of the heavy

41

work load the doctor carried and of the extra working hours necessary in each day for the doctor to study case histories of new patients. He had to read the latest journals and write his own occasional articles for those same prestigious publications. It was clear that Miss Pringle somewhat idolized him, and Chase wondered whether she slept with him. In all the times he had seen her, such a thought had never occurred to him. Uneasily, he realized that it was a sign of changing circumstances – changes in his life utterly beyond his control. But perhaps they were not beyond the doctor's control. When she was halfway through her set speech, having recovered a bit of her plastic, warm tone of friendship, Chase interrupted her, and in a few well-chosen words, convinced her to ask Dr Cauvel himself.

A few minutes later, chagrined, Miss Pringle returned to the phone to tell Chase he had an appointment for four o'clock that same afternoon. Clearly, she was perturbed that the rules should be broken for him. She must have known that the government paid the tab and that Cauvel received less compensation for his time than he would have by indulging a wealthy neurotic. What she had quite forgotten to include in her detailed schedule of the doctor's day, however, was time to have extra sessions with patients whom the doctor considered especially intriguing.

It helped, if one had to be slightly mad, to have a very unique sort of madness . . .

At eleven-thirty, while Chase was dressing to go out for lunch, Judge called again. His voice sounded better, though still not normal. He said, 'How are you feeling this morning?'

'Well,' Chase said, though that was a lie.

'Be expecting a call at six this evening,' Judge said.

'Look here –'

'At six o'clock sharp, Mr Chase. Do you understand me?' He spoke with the smooth authority of a man accustomed to being obeyed. 'I will have several interesting points to discuss with you, I'm sure.'

'I understand,' Chase said.

Judge said, 'Have a good day, now.'

They broke the connection at the same moment. Chase slammed his receiver into its cradle. Hard.

The room on the eighth floor of the Kaine Building, in the centre of the city, did not resemble a psychiatrist's counselling chamber as the image had been established in countless films and books. For one thing, it was not small and intimate, not at all reminiscent of the womb. It was a pleasant, musty, rambling chamber, perhaps thirty feet by thirty-five, with a high and shadow-shrouded ceiling. Two of the walls contained bookshelves that ran from floor to ceiling; one wall was dressed with paintings depicting tranquil country scenes, while the fourth wall was nothing but white plaster and two large windows. The bookshelves contained only a handful of expensively bound volumes, along with close to three hundred glass dogs, none larger than the palm of a man's hand and most a good deal smaller than that. Collecting glass dogs was Dr Cauvel's hobby.

Just as the room – with its battered desk, heavily padded easy chairs and foot-scarred coffee table – did not look its purpose, Dr Cauvel was as unlike any stereotypical image of a psychiatrist as was possible, whether by intent or nature Chase never knew for certain. He was a small man, rather athletic-looking, with hair that spilled over his collar in a manner that suggested carelessness rather than style. He always looked as if he needed a shave, and he always wore a blue suit cut a bit too long in the trousers and in need of a hot iron. It was possible to see him as a schoolteacher (English), a store manager (the local five-and-ten), or the minister of some esoteric fundamentalist Christian sect. But not a doctor. And not ever, ever a doctor of the mind.

'Sit down, Ben,' Cauvel said. 'Like a drink?'

'No, thank you,' Chase said. There was no couch upon which to act out the familiar scene of psychiatry's myths. Chase sat in his favourite easy chair.

Cauvel took the chair to Chase's right, sank back and propped his feet on the coffee table. He urged Chase to follow suit. When they were at least in the pose of relaxation, he said, 'No preliminaries, then?'

'Not today,' Chase said.

'You're tense, Ben.'

'Yes.' Chase tried to determine where he should begin, how the story should be best unfolded.

'Tell me about it?'

Now, Chase clearly remembered the first time Judge had called him, but he could not bring himself to explain the situation to Cauvel. Even making this appointment had been an admission of his slowly dissolving hold on things: explaining it might be ruinous.

'Can't do it?'

'No.'

'Want to play some word association?'

Chase nodded, dreading the game they often used to loosen his tongue. He always seemed to expose more of himself than he wished in his answers. And Cauvel did not play it according to established rules, but with a swift and vicious tone that cut quickly to the heart of the matter. Still, he said, 'Go on.'

Cauvel said, 'Mother.'

'Dead.'

'Father.'

'Dead.'

Cauvel had his fingers steepled before him, like a child playing the See the Church game. 'Love.'

'Woman.'

'Love.'

'Woman,' Chase repeated.

Cauvel did not look at him but stared studiously at the blue glass terrier on the bookshelf nearest him. He said, 'Don't repeat yourself, please.' When Chase had apologized (he had been surprised the first time Cauvel had expected an apology, for he had not thought such a guilt-touched relationship was desirable between a psychiatrist and his patient; with each enusing apology over the months, he was less surprised at anything Cauvel might suggest), the doctor said, 'Love.'

'Girl.'

'That's an evasion.'

'Everything is an evasion.'

That observation appeared to surprise the doctor, but not enough to jar him out of the stubborn, wearying routine which he had begun. He said, after a slight pause, 'Love.'

Already Chase was perspiring, and he did not know why. He finally said, 'Myself.'

'Very good,' Cauvel said. And now the interchange of words went faster, one barked close after the other, as if speed counted in the scoring. Cauvel said, 'Hate.'

'Army.'

'Hate.'

'Vietnam.'

'Hate!' Cauvel raised his voice, almost shouted it.

'Guns.'

'*Hate*!'

'Zacharia,' Chase said, though he had often sworn never to repeat that name again or to remember the man attached to it or, indeed, to recall the events that man had perpetrated.

'Hate,' Cauvel said, more quietly this time.

'Another word, please.'

'Hate,' Cauvel insisted.

'Lieutenant Zacharia, Lieutenant Zacharia, Lieutenant Zacharia!'

Abruptly, the doctor brought an end to the game, though it had been much less complex than usual. He said, 'Do you remember what Lieutenant Zacharia ordered you to do, Benjamin?'

'Yes, sir.'

'What were those orders?'

'We had sealed off the two back entrances to a Cong tunnel system, and Lieutenant Zacharia ordered me to clear the last entrance.'

'How did you accomplish that?'

'With a grenade, sir. Then, before the air round the

tunnel face could clear, I went forward and used a machine gun.'

'Then, Benjamin?'

'Then we went down, sir.'

'We?'

'Lieutenant Zacharia, Sergeant Coombs, Privates Halsey and Wade, a couple of other men.'

'And you.'

'Yes, and me.'

'Then?'

'In the tunnels, we found four dead men and parts of men lying in the foyer of the complex. Lieutenant Zacharia ordered a cautious advance. A hundred and fifty yards along, we came across a bamboo grate behind which a number of villagers, mostly women, were stationed.'

'How many women, Ben?'

'Maybe twenty.'

'Children?'

Chase sank down in the heavy padding, his shoulders drawn up as if he wished to hide between them. 'A few.'

'Then?'

'We tried to open the grate, but the women were holding it shut with a system of ropes. When we ordered them out of the way, they would not move. The lieutenant said it might very well be a trap, designed to contain us at that point until the Cong could somehow get behind us. It was dark. There was a smell in that tunnel I can't explain, made up of sweat and urine and rotting vegetables, as heavy as if it had substance. Lieutenant Zacharia ordered us to open fire and clear the way.'

'Did you comply?'

'Yes. Everyone did.'

'Later, when the tunnel had been demolished, you ran into the ambush which earned you your Medal of Honor.'

'Yes,' Chase said.

Cauvel said, 'You crawled across the field of fire for a distance of nearly two hundred yards and brought back a wounded sergeant named Coombs. You received two minor but painful wounds in the thigh and calf of your right leg, but you did not stop crawling until you had reached shelter, at which point you secured Coombs behind a stand of scrub, and having reached a point on the enemy's flank by means of your heroic crossing of the open field, accounted for eighteen communist soldiers. Your actions, therefore, not only saved Sergeant Coombs' life but contributed substantially to the well-being of your entire unit.' He had only slightly paraphrased the wording on the scroll which Chase had received in the mail from the President himself.

Chase said nothing.

'You see where this heroism came from, Ben?'

'We've talked about it before. It came from guilt, because I wanted to die, subconsciously wanted to be killed.'

'Do you believe that analysis, or do you think it's just something I made up to degrade your medal?'

Chase said, 'I believe it. I never wanted the medal in the first place.'

'Now,' Cauvel said, unsteepling his fingers, 'lets extend that analysis just a bit. Though you hoped to be shot and killed in that ambush, took absurd risks to make it a certainty, the opposite transpired. You became a national hero. When you learned Lieutenant Zacharia had submitted your name for consideration, you suffered a nervous breakdown that hospitalized you and eventually led to your honourable discharge. The breakdown was an attempt to punish yourself, once you'd failed to get yourself killed, but it failed too. Well regarded, honourably discharged, too strong not to recover from the breakdown, you still carried your burden of guilt.'

There was a pause. Chase was silent.

Cauvel continued: 'Perhaps when you chanced upon that scene in the park on Kanackaway, you recognized another opportunity to punish yourself. You must have realized that there was a strong possibility that you would be hurt or killed, and you must have subconsciously anticipated that agreeably enough.'

'You're wrong,' Chase said. 'It wasn't like that at all. I had thirty pounds on him, and I knew what I was doing. He was an amateur. He had no hope of really hurting me.'

Cauvel said nothing. Several minutes passed until Chase recognized the scene they were acting out and had acted out in a number of other sessions. When he apologized at last, Cauvel smiled at him. 'Well, you aren't a psychiatrist, so we can't expect you to see into it quite so clearly. You aren't detached from it like I am.' He cleared his throat, looked back at the blue terrier. He said, 'Now that we have come this far, why did you solicit this extra session, Ben?'

Once he began, Chase found the telling easy. In ten

minutes he had related the events of the previous day and repeated, almost word for word, the conversations he had with Judge.

When he had finished, Cauvel asked, 'What do you want of me, then?'

'I want to know how to handle it, some advice. When he calls, it's more than just the threats that upset me. It's – a feeling of detachment from everything, like I was in the hospital.'

'Another breakdown?'

'I'm afraid there might be.'

Cauvel said, 'My advice is to ignore him.'

'I can't.'

'You must,' Cauvel said.

'What if he's serious? What if he's really going to kill me?'

'He won't.'

'How can you be sure?' Chase was perspiring heavily. Great dark circles stained the underarms of his shirt and plastered it to his back.

Cauvel smiled at the blue terrier, shifted his gaze to a greyhound blown in amber, that smug, self-assured look drifting over his face like a mask. 'I can be so sure of that, because Judge does not exist.'

For a moment Chase did not understand the reply. When he grasped the import of it, he did not like it. He said, 'How could I have hallucinated it? The part about the murder and the girl are in the papers.'

'Oh, that was real enough,' Cauvel said. 'But these phone calls are all so much illusion.'

'It can't be.'

Cauvel ignored that and said, 'I've noticed for some time that you have begun to shake off this unnatural desire for privacy and that you're facing the world a little bit more squarely on, week by week. You've felt yourself growing curious about the rest of the world, and you've become restless to *do* something. Is that correct?'

'I don't know,' Chase said. But he did know, it was correct, and it bothered him that it was so.

'Perhaps you even felt a renewal of your sexual urge, but perhaps not that much yet. A counter-reaction of guilt set in, because you had not yet been punished for the things that happened in that tunnel, and you didn't want to lead a normal life until you felt you'd suffered enough.'

Chase said nothing. He disliked the tone of smug complacency, of unquestioned self-assurance that Cauvel adopted for moments like this. Right now all he wanted was out of there, to get home and close the door and open the bottle. A new bottle.

Cauvel said, 'You couldn't accept the fact that you wanted to taste the good things of life again, and you invented Judge because he represented the remaining possibility of punishment. You had to make some excuses for being forced into life again, and Judge worked well in this respect too. You would, sooner or later, have to take the initiative to stop him. You could pretend that you still wanted seclusion in which to mourn but were no longer being permitted that indulgence.'

'All wrong,' Chase said, 'Judge is real.'

'I think not.' Cauvel smiled at the amber greyhound and said, 'If you thought he was real, why not go to the the police rather than your psychiatrist?'

Chase had no answer. He said, 'You're twisting things.'

51

'No. Just showing you the straight truth.' He stood up, stretched, his too-long trousers rising on his unpolished shoes, falling when he finished his yawn. 'I recommend you go home and forget Judge. You don't need an excuse to live like a normal human being. You *have* suffered enough, Ben, more than enough. For the lives you took, you saved others. Remember that.'

Chase stood, bewildered, no longer perfectly sure that he did know what was real and what was not. Cauvel put his arm around his shoulder and walked him to the door.

'Friday at three,' the doctor said. 'Let's see how far out of your hole you've come by then. I think you're going to make it, Ben. Don't despair.'

Miss Pringle escorted him to the outer door of the waiting room and closed it after him, leaving him alone in the hallway.

'Judge is real,' Chase said to no one at all. 'Isn't he?'

Four

Chase was sitting on the edge of his bed by the nightstand where the telephone stood, sipping at his second glass of Jack Daniel's, when six o'clock rolled around. He put the drink down and wiped his sweaty hands on his slacks, cleared his throat so that his voice would not catch when he tried to speak.

At 6:05 he began to feel uneasy. He thought of going downstairs to ask Mrs Fiedling what time her clocks read, in the event that his own was not functioning properly. He refrained from that only because he was afraid of missing the call if it should come while he was down there.

At 6:15 he picked up his drink again and sipped at it steadily, watching the phone as if it might try to move. His hands were damp again; beads of perspiration had appeared on his forehead.

At 6:30 he went to the cupboard, took down his whisky bottle of the day – which had barely been

53

touched – and poured his third glass. He did not put it away again, but left it out on the waist-high cupboard counter where he could easily reach it. He read the label, which he had studied a hundred times before, then carried his drink back to the bed.

By seven o'clock he was feeling all the liquor in him. Everything had become softened, his movements lethargic. He settled back against the headboard and finally faced the truth: Cauvel had been correct. There was no Judge. Judge had been an illusion, a psychological mechanism for rationalization of his slowly lessening guilt complex. He tried to think about that, to study the meaning of it, but he could not be sure if this was a good or a bad development.

In the bathroom, he drew a tub of warm water and tested it with his hand until it was just right. He folded a damp washcloth over the wide porcelain rim of the tub and placed his drink on that, stripped, stepped into the tub and settled down until, seated, the water came partway up his chest. It was very nice, comforting. The whisky and the water and the steam rising around him had all conspired to make him feel as if he were floating, falling *up* into a stream of soft clouds. He leaned back until his head touched the wall, closed his eyes and tried not to think about anything – especially about Judge and the Medal of Honor and the nine months he had spent on active duty in Nam.

Unfortunately, he began to think of Louise Allenby, the girl whose life he had saved, and his mind was filled with a vision of her small, trembling, bare breasts which had looked so inviting in the weak light of the car in lover's lane. The thought, though pleasant enough, was unfortunate because it contributed to his first erection in nearly a year. That development, while desirable, was both startling and familiar enough to make him recall all the barren months when he had harboured no desire. It also brought back the reasons for his previous inability to function as a man, and those reasons were still so huge and formidable that he could not face them alone. The erection was short-lived, and when it was gone altogether, he could not be certain if it indicated an end to his psychological impotency or whether it had stemmed only from the warm water, a reaction of dumb nerves rather than sensitive emotions.

He only got out of the water when there was no more whisky in his glass, and he was drying himself when the telephone rang.

The electric clock read 8:00.

Naked, he sat down and picked up the phone.

'Sorry I'm late,' Judge said.

Dr Cauvel had been wrong.

'I thought you weren't going to call,' Chase said.

'Would I let you down?' Judge asked, mock hurt in his tone. 'It was just that I required a little more time to locate some information on you.'

'What information?'

Judge ignored the question, intent on proceeding in his own fashion. 'So you see a psychiatrist once a week, do you? That alone is fairly good proof that the accusation I made yesterday is true – that your disability pension is for mental injuries, not physical ones.'

Chase wished that he had a drink with him, but he could not ask Judge to hold on while he poured himself one. For some reason he could not explain, he did not want Judge to know that he drank heavily.

Chase said, 'How did you find out?'

'Followed you this afternoon,' Judge said.

'You don't have the right to –'

Judge laughed. He said, 'I saw you going into the Kaine Building, and I got into the lobby fast enough to see what elevator you took and which floor you got off at. On the eighth floor, besides Dr Cauvel's offices, there are two dentists, three insurance companies and a tax collection office. It was simple enough to look in the waiting rooms of those other places or to inquire after you, like a friend, with the secretaries and receptionists. I left the head doctor's place for last, because I just *knew* that's where you were. When no one knew of you in the other offices, I didn't even have to risk looking in Cauvel's waiting room. I knew.'

Chase said, 'So what?'

He hoped that he sounded more nonchalant than he felt, for it was somehow important to make the right impression on Judge. He was sweating again. He would need to take another bath by the time this conversation was concluded. And he would need a drink, a cold drink.

'Let me tell you why I was late calling,' Judge said.

'Go on.'

'As soon as I knew for sure you were in the psychiatrist's office, I was aware of the necessity to obtain copies of his personal files on you. I decided to remain in the building, out of sight, until all the offices were closed and the employees had gone home.'

'I don't believe you,' Chase said, aware of what was coming, dreading to hear it.

'You don't *want* to believe me, but you do. Now let me explain how it was.' Judge took a long, slow breath before he continued: 'The eighth floor was clear by six o'clock. By six-thirty I managed to get the door open into Dr Cauvel's suite. I know a little about such things, and I was careful; I did not damage the lock, and I didn't trip any alarms because there were none. I required an additional half an hour to locate his files and to secure your records, which I copied on his own photocopier.'

'Breaking and entering – then theft,' Chase said.

'But it hardly matters on top of what the authorities would consider murder, does it?'

Chase had no reply.

'You'll receive in the mail, probably the day after tomorrow, complete copies of Dr Cauvel's notes on you, along with copies of several articles he had written for various medical journals. You're mentioned in all these and are, in some of them, the sole subject of discussion.'

Chase said, 'I didn't know he'd done that.'

'They're interesting articles, Chase. They'll give you some idea of what he thinks of you.' Judge's tone changed then, became far more haughty and was touched with contempt. 'Reading those records, Chase, I found more than enough to permit me to pass judgment on you.'

'Oh?'

'I read all about how you got your Medal of Honor.'

Chase waited.

'And I read about the tunnels and what you did in those – and how you helped Lieutenant Zacharia to cover the evidence and falsify the eventual report. Do you think the Congress would have voted you the Medal of Honor if they had known you killed civilians, Chase?'

'Stop it.'

'You killed women, didn't you?'

'I said stop it.'

'You killed women and children, Chase, noncombatants.'

'You son of a bitch.'

'Children, Chase. You killed children. What kind of animal are you, Chase?'

'*Shut up!*' Chase had come to his feet as if something had exploded close behind him. 'What would you know about it? Were you ever over there, did you ever have to serve in that stinking country?'

'Some patriotic paean to duty won't change my mind, Chase. We all love this country, but most of us realize there are limits to –'

'Bullshit,' Chase said.

He could not remember having been this angry in all the time since his breakdown. Now and then he had been irritated by something or someone, but never driven to the extremes of emotion.

'Chase –'

'I bet you were all for the war. I'll bet you're one of the hawks that made it possible for me to be there in the first place. It's easy to set standards of performance, select limits of right and wrong, when you never get closer than ten thousand miles to the place where it's all coming down!'

Judge attempted to comment but could not break in.

Chase said, 'I didn't even *want* to be there. I didn't believe in it, and I was scared shitless the whole time. Mostly, all I thought about was staying alive. In that tunnel, I couldn't think of anything else. I wasn't *me*. I was a textbook case of paranoia. And now, dammit, I won't let you or anyone else blame *me* for what a textbook example did!'

'You do feel guilty, though,' Judge observed.

'That doesn't matter.'

'I think it does.'

'It *doesn't* matter, because no matter how guilty I feel you haven't the right to pass judgment on me. You're sitting there with your little list of commandments, but you've never been anywhere that made a list seem pointless, anywhere that the environment forced you into reacting in a manner you loathed.' Chase found, amazingly, that he was crying. He had not cried in a long time.

'You're rationalizing,' Judge began, trying to regain control of the conversation.

Chase would not permit that. He said, 'And remember that you've not followed that commandment yourself. You killed that boy, that Michael Karnes.'

'There was a difference,' Judge said. Some of the hoarseness had returned to his voice.

'Oh?'

'Yes,' Judge said, on the defensive now. 'I studied his situation carefully, collected evidence against him, and only then passed judgment. You didn't do any of that, Chase. You killed perfect strangers, and you very likely murdered innocents who had no black marks on their souls.'

CHASE

Chase slammed the phone down.

When it rang at four different times during the following hour, he was able to ignore it completely. His anger remained sharp, the strongest emotion he had experienced in long months of near-catatonia.

He drank three more glasses of whisky before he began to feel a bit mellow again. His anger had burned up all traces of the drunkenness which his first few drinks had brought. The tremors slowly stilled in his hands.

At ten o'clock he dialled the number of the police headquarters and asked for Detective Wallace, who at that moment was out. He dressed, drank another glass of Jack Daniel's and tried again at 10:40. This time Wallace was in and willing to speak to him.

'Nothing's going as well as we hoped,' Wallace said. 'He doesn't seem to have been printed. At least, the prints on that knife don't match up with anything in federal or state files.'

'They could have checked the files this quickly?'

'Yeah,' Wallace said. 'They have computers that scan and compare much faster than a team of investigators could – something like the computers that read handwriting and sort mail at post offices.'

'What about the ring?'

'Turns out to be a cheap accessory that sells at under fifteen bucks retail in about every store in the state. Impossible to keep track of where and when and to whom a certain ring might be sold.'

Chase committed himself reluctantly. 'Then I have something for you,' he said. In a few short sentences he told the detective about Judge's calls.

Wallace was plainly angry, though he made an

effort not to shout. 'Why in the hell didn't you let us know about his before?'

'I thought, with the prints, you'd be sure to get him.'

'Prints hardly ever make a difference in a situation like this,' Wallace said. There was still a bite in his voice, though it was muted now. He had evidently taken a moment to consider the stature of his informant.

'Besides,' Chase said, 'the killer realized the chance of the line being tapped. He's been calling from pay phones and keeping the calls under five minutes.'

Wallace said, 'Just the same, I'd like to hear him. I'll be over with a man in fifteen minutes.'

'Just one man?'

Wallace said, 'We'll try not to upset your routine too much.'

Chase almost laughed at that. He said, 'I'll be waiting.'

The man who came with Wallace was introduced as James Tuppinger, and he was not said to have any rank with the police department, though Chase figured him as Wallace's equal. He was six inches taller than the detective and not so grey and ordinary-looking. He wore his blond hair in such a short crew cut that he appeared almost bald from a distance. His eyes were blue and moved from object to object with the swift, penetrating glance of an accountant itemizing an inventory. He carried a large suitcase in his right hand and didn't put it down when he offered Chase his left.

Mrs Fiedling watched from the living room, where

she pretended to be engrossed in a television programme, but she did not come out to see what was going on. Chase got the two of them upstairs before she could learn who they were.

'Cozy little place you have,' Wallace said.

'It's enough for me,' Chase said.

Tuppinger's eyes flicked about, catching the unmade bed, the couple of dirty whisky glasses on the cupboard, the bottle of liquor which was nearly half empty. He did not say anything. He took his suitcase full of tools to the phone, put it down, and began examining the lead-in wires that came through the wall near the base of the single window.

While Tuppinger worked, Wallace questioned Chase. 'What did he sound like on the phone?'

'Hard to say.'

'Old? Young?'

'In between.'

'Accent?'

'No.'

'Speech impediment?'

'No,' Chase said. 'At first, though, he was hoarse – apparently from the strangling I gave him.'

Wallace said, 'Can you remember what he said, each time he called?'

'Approximately.'

'Tell me, then.' He slumped down in the only easy chair in the room and crossed his legs before him. He looked as if he had fallen asleep, though he was only conserving his energy while he waited.

Chase told him everything that he could remember about the strange conversations with Judge, then revealed some things he had forgotten as Wallace asked a few more probing questions.

'He sounds like a religious psychotic,' Wallace said. 'All this stuff about fornication and sin and passing judgments.'

'Maybe,' Chase said. 'But I wouldn't look for him at tent meetings. I think it's more of a moral excuse to kill than a genuine belief.'

'Maybe,' Wallace said. 'Then again, we get his sort every once in a while, more regularly than any other brand of madman.'

Five minutes later, as Wallace and Chase sat in silence, Tuppinger finished his work. He explained his listening and recording equipment to Chase and further explained the tracery network the telephone company had in use to seek Judge when he called.

'Well,' Wallace said, 'tonight I intend to go home when I'm supposed to.' Just the thought of eight hours' sleep brought his lids down further and increased the red tint in his eyes.

'One thing,' Chase said.

'What's that?'

'If this leads to something – do you have to tell the press about my part in it?'

'Why?' Wallace asked.

'It's just that I'm tired of being a celebrity, of having people bother me all hours of the day and night.'

'It has to come out at the trial, if we nab him,' Wallace said.

'But not before?'

'I guess not.'

'I'd appreciate it,' Chase said. 'In any case, I'll have to appear at the trial, won't I?'

'Probably.'

'So, if the press didn't have to know until then, it would cut down on the news coverage by half.'

'You're really modest, aren't you?' Wallace asked. Before Chase could respond to that, the detective smiled, clapped him on the shoulder and left.

'Would you like a drink?' Chase asked Tuppinger.

'Not on duty.'

'Mind if I–?'

'No. Go ahead.'

Chase noticed that Tuppinger watched him with interest as he got new ice cubes and poured himself a large dose of whisky. It wasn't as large as usual. He supposed he'd have to restrain his thirst a bit with the policeman around.

When Chase sat on the bed, Tuppinger said, 'I read all about your exploits over there.'

'Oh?'

'Really something,' Tuppinger said.

'Not really.'

'Oh, yes, really,' Tuppinger insisted. He was sitting in the easy chair, which he had moved close to his equipment. 'It had to be hard over there, worse than anybody at home could ever know.'

Chase nodded.

'I'd imagine the medals don't mean that much. I mean, considering how much you had to go through to earn them, they must seem kind of insignificant.'

Chase looked up from his drink, surprised at the insight. 'You're right,' he said. 'They don't mean anything.'

Tuppinger said, 'And it must be hard to come back from a place like that and settle into a normal life. Memories couldn't fade that quickly.'

CHASE

Chase started to respond, then saw that Tuppinger was looking meaningfully at the glass of whisky in his hand. He closed his mouth, bit off his response. Then, hating Tuppinger as badly as he hated Judge, he lifted the drink and took a very large swallow of it.

He said, 'I'll have another, I think. You sure you don't want one?'

'Positive,' Tuppinger said.

When Chase returned to the bed with another glassful, Tuppinger cautioned him against answering the phone without first waiting for the tape to be started. Then he went into the bathroom, where he remained almost ten minutes.

When he came back, Chase asked, 'How late do we have to stay up?'

'Has he ever called this late – except that first night?'

'No,' Chase said.

'Then I'll turn in now,' Tuppinger said, flopping in the easy chair. 'See you in the morning.'

In the morning the whispers of the dead men woke Chase, but they turned out to be nothing more than the sound of water running in the bathroom sink. Tuppinger had risen first and was shaving. When he opened the door and came out a few minutes later, looking refreshed, he nodded at Chase. 'All yours!' He seemed remarkably energetic for having spent the night in the easy chair.

Chase took his time bathing and shaving, for the longer he remained in the bathroom, the less he would have to talk to the cop. When he was finally finished, the clock by his bed read 9:45. Judge had not yet called.

'What have you got for breakfast?' Tuppinger asked.

Chase said, 'There isn't anything here.'

'Oh, you've got to have something. Doesn't have to be breakfast food; I'm not particular in the morning.'

Chase opened the refrigerator and took out the bag of Winesap apples. He said, 'Only these.'

Tuppinger stared at the apples, at the empty refrigerator. His eyes flicked to the whisky bottle on the cupboard. He did not say anything, for he did not *need* to say anything. Indeed, if he had remarked according to his thoughts, Chase might have struck him.

'They'll do fine,' Tuppinger said enthusiastically. He took the clear plastic bag from Chase and chose an apple. 'Want one?'

'No.'

'You ought to eat breakfast,' Tuppinger said. 'Even something small. Gets the stomach working, sharpens you up for the day ahead.'

'No thanks,' Chase said.

'Tuppinger carefully peeled two apples, sectioned them and ate them slowly, chewing well.

By 10:30 Chase was beginning to worry. Suppose Judge did not call today? The idea of having Tuppinger here for the afternoon and the evening, of waking up to the sound of Tuppinger in the bathroom shaving, was all but intolerable.

'Do you have a relief man?' Chase asked.

'Unless it gets too protracted,' Tuppinger said, 'I'll stick with it myself.'

'How long might that be?'

'Oh,' Tuppinger said, 'if we don't have it wrapped up in forty-eight hours, I'll call in my relief.'

Though another forty-eight hours with Tuppinger was in no way an attractive prospect, it was probably no worse, and perhaps better, than it would have been with another cop. Though Tuppinger was a bit too observant for comfort, he did not talk very much. Let him look, then. And let him think whatever he wanted to think about Chase. So long as he could keep his mouth shut, they wouldn't have any major problems.

At noon Tuppinger had two more apples and cajoled Chase into eating most of one. It was decided that Chase would go out for some fried chicken and slaw to bring back for supper.

At 12:30 Chase had his first drink.

Tuppinger watched, but he did not say anything.

Chase didn't offer him a drink this time.

At three in the afternoon the telephone rang. Although this was what they had been waiting for since the night before, Chase did not want to answer it. Because Tuppinger was there, urging him to pick it up while he adjusted his own earphones, he finally lifted the receiver.

'Hello?' His voice sounded cracked, strained.

'Mr Chase?'

'Yes,' he said, immediately recognizing the voice. It was not Judge.

'This is Miss Pringle, calling for Dr Cauvel, to remind you of your appointment tomorrow at three. You have a fifty-minute session scheduled, as usual.'

'Thank you,' he said. This double-check was a strict routine with Miss Pringle, though he had forgotten about it.

'Tomorrow at three,' she repeated, then hung up.

At four o'clock Tuppinger complained of hunger and of a reluctance to consume a fifth Winesap apple in order to stave it off. Chase did not object to an early supper, accepted Tuppinger's money, which, the cop said, would be paid him from the petty-cash account at headquarters, and went out to buy the chicken, French fries and slaw. He purchased a large Coca-Cola for Tuppinger but nothing for himself. He would drink his usual.

They ate at twenty minutes to five, not bothering with dinner conversation, watching the silent phone.

Two hours later Wallace arrived, looking thoroughly weary though he had only come on duty at six, less than an hour earlier. He said, 'Mr Chase, do you think I might have a word, alone, with Jim?'

'Sure,' Chase said. He stepped into the bathroom and closed the door. As an afterthought, he turned on the water in the sink and listened to the dead men whisper, though the noise put him on edge. He lowered the lid of the commode and sat down facing the empty bathtub, and he saw that it needed to be scrubbed out. He wondered if Tuppinger had noticed.

Less than five minutes passed before Wallace knocked on the door. He said, 'Sorry to have pushed you out of your own place like that.' He smiled as if they were being very conspiratorial, and said, 'Police business.'

Chase said, 'We haven't been lucky, as Tuppinger may have told you.'

Wallace nodded. He looked peculiarly sheepish, and for the first time he could not meet Chase's gaze. 'I've heard,' he said.

'It's the longest he's gone without calling.'

Wallace nodded. 'It's possible, you know, that he won't be calling at all, now.'

'You mean, since he passed judgment on me?'

Wallace said nothing, backed into the living room and turned to look at Tuppinger. When Chase followed, he saw that the other man was disconnecting wires and packing his equipment into the suitcase. Wallace said, 'I'm afraid you're right, Mr Chase. The killer has passed his judgment, and he isn't going to try to contact you again. We don't want to keep a man tied up –'

'You're leaving?' Chase asked.

Wallace did not even look in his direction. 'Yes,' he said.

'But another few hours might –'

'Might produce nothing,' Wallace said. 'What we're going to do, Mr Chase, is we're going to rely on you to tell us what Judge says if, as seems unlikely now, he should call again.' He smiled at Chase.

In that smile was all the explanation that Chase required. He said, 'When Tuppinger sent me out for supper, he called you, didn't he?' Not waiting for a response, he went on: 'And he told you about the call from Dr Cauvel's secretary – the word "session" probably sparked him. And now you've talked to the good doctor.'

Tuppinger finished packing the equipment and stood up. He hefted the case and looked quickly about the room to be sure he had not left anything behind.

'Judge is real,' Chase told Wallace.

'I'm sure that he is,' Wallace said. 'That's why I

want you to report any calls he might make to you.'
But his tone was that of an adult pretending with an
adolescent.

'You stupid bastard, he *is* real!'

Wallace coloured from the neck up. When he
spoke, there was tension in his voice, and the even
tone was false. He said, 'Mr Chase, you saved the girl,
and you deserve to be praised for that. But the fact
remains that no one has called here in nearly
twenty-four hours. Also fact: if you believed such a
man as Judge existed, you would have contacted us
before this, after he first called. It was only natural to
respond that way – especially for a duty-conscious
young man like yourself. These things, examined in
the light of your psychiatric record and Dr Cauvel's
explanations, make it clear that the expenditure of
one of our best men is not now required. Tuppinger
has other duties.'

Chase could see how overwhelmingly the evidence
seemed to point to Dr Cauvel's thesis, just as he could
see how his own behaviour – his fondness for whisky
in front of Tuppinger, his inability to carry on a
conversation, his anxiety to avoid publicity that might
have appeared the protestation of a man who wanted
just the opposite – could have reinforced it. Still, with
his fists balled at his sides, he said, 'Get out.'

'Take it easy, son,' Wallace said.

'Get out, now.'

Wallace looked around the room and let his eyes
stop on the bottle of whisky. He said, 'Tuppinger tells
me you haven't any food on hand, but that there are
five bottles in that cupboard.' He did not look at
Chase; he seemed to be embarrassed both by

Tuppinger's obvious spying and by his own inability to sympathize properly with another human being. He said, 'You look thirty pounds underweight, son.'

'Get out,' Chase said. He did not want to shout and draw Mrs Fiedling's attention. but he could not think of any other way to make Wallace listen to him.

Wallace was not ready to leave yet. He was searching for some way to make his departure seem more warranted, and he looked as if he might tell Chase how understaffed they were down at police headquarters. He avoided that cliché, though, and said, 'No matter what happened to you over there, in Vietnam, you aren't going to forget about it with whisky. Don't drink so much.' Before Chase, infuriated at the homespun psychoanalysis, could order him out again, Wallace left with Tuppinger at his heels.

Chase slammed the door after them, went to the cupboard and poured himself a drink. He was alone again. But he was used to that.

Five

Thursday evening at seven-thirty, having successfully evaded Mrs Fiedling on his way out of the house, Chase got in his Mustang and drove toward Kanackaway Ridge Road, aware and yet unaware of his destination. He drove well within the speed limits through Ashside and the outlying districts, but floored the accelerator at the bottom of the mountain road, taking the wide curves on the far outside, the white guardrails slipping past so quickly and so close on the right that they blurred into one continuous wall of pale planking, the cables between them like black scrawls on the phantom boards.

On the top of the ridge highway, he parked at the same spot he had been on Monday night, shut off the motor and leaned back in his seat, listening to the soft wind. He realized at once that he should never have stopped, that he should have kept moving at all costs. As long as he was moving, he did not have to wonder what he was going to do next, for he could easily lose himself in the pace of his driving. Stopped, he was perplexed, frustrated.

He opened the door and got out of the car, uncertain what he expected to find out here that would be of any help to him. A good hour or so of daylight remained in which to search the area where the Chevy had been parked. Even so, the police would have combed and recombed it far more thoroughly than he ever could. At least, out of the car, he could walk about, move, and therefore stop thinking unpleasant thoughts.

He strolled along the park edge and then across to the row of brambles where the Chevy had sat. The sod was well tramped, littered with half-smoked cigarette butts, candy wrappers and balled-up pages from a reporter's note pad. He kicked at the debris, scanning the mashed grass, and he felt silly. He might just as well attempt to estimate the number of sightseers who had flocked to the murder scene as to try hunting for a clue in all this mess. The results would probably be more rewarding, if esoteric.

Next, he walked to the railing at the cliff's edge and leaned against it, staring down the jumbled wall of rock at the tangled patch of brambles and locust trees below. When he raised his head, he could see the entire city spread along the valley, but especially the green copper plating of the courthouse dome.

He was still looking at that corroded curve of metal when he heard a peculiar whining sound and felt the rail beneath his hands shiver. Looking to either side, seeing no one, he was about to dismiss it when he heard and felt the same thing again. This time, leaning over the precipice, he recognized the source: a bullet slapping the iron pipe and ricocheting away.

With a quickness honed in combat, he whirled and fell back from the rail and the rim of the cliff. As he dropped to the ground, he evaluated the parkland nearby and chose the nearest decorative wall of brambles as the most likely point of safety. He rolled toward them and came up against the thorns so hard he tore his cheek and forehead on them. Then he lay quite still, waiting.

A minute passed, then another, with no sound but the wind.

Chase crawled on his stomach, working his way to the far end of the bramble row that paralleled the highway at this point. When he got there, he moved slowly into the open, scanning the ground toward the highway for some sign of the man who had shot at him. The park seemed deserted.

He started to get up, then fell back again, more out of instinct than cunning. Where he had been, the grass was parted by a bullet that kicked up a puff of earth. Whoever was after him had a pistol with a silencer attached.

For a moment he considered the implausibility of anyone in civilian life having access to a silencer. Even in Nam, where officers requisitioned unnecessary weapons for black market sale and for shipping home to their own addresses for sale after the war, silencers were not that common. For one thing, most soldiers who carried handguns much preferred the revolver for its higher degree of accuracy and the lesser likelihood that it would jam at a crucial moment. Revolvers could not be silenced effectively, but no

one in Nam much cared about the noise of a shot. To
own a silenced pistol in civilian life was testament to
illegal activity of some sort, and one could not
purchase the fixture in just any gunshop.

He took no time at all to wonder who could be firing
at him, for he had known at once who was out there.
Judge, of course.

Turning, he scrambled back along the twisting
brambles to a point midway in the length of the row.
Swiftly he unbuttoned his shirt and took it off, tore it
into two pieces and wrapped his hands with the cloth.
Lying on his stomach, he carefully pressed the thorny
vines apart until he had opened a chink through which
he could survey the immediate land beyond.

He saw Judge almost at once. The man was huddled
by the front fender of Chase's Mustang, down on one
knee, the pistol held out at arm's length as he waited
for his prey to appear. Two hundred feet away, in the
weak, last light of the evening, he was fairly well
shielded from Chase, little more than a dark figure
with a blur of a face, cut over with confusing swaths of
shadow.

Chase let the brambles go and stripped the cloth
from his hands. He had nicked the tips of his fingers in
a few places, but he was for the most part unscathed.

To his right, no more than four feet away, a bullet
snapped through the brambles, spraying pieces of
vinery, and went on, hissing once as it skipped on the
concrete walkway by the cliff railing. Another passed
at the level of Chase's head, no more than two feet on
his left, and then another still farther along the row.
Judge did not have the nerves of a professional killer,
and obviously tired of waiting, had begun to fire

blindly in hopes of making a lucky hit.

Chase smiled and began to crawl slowly back toward the right-hand end of the row.

When he got there, he peered cautiously out and saw Judge standing up, leaning against the car, attempting to reload his pistol. His head was bent over his task, and though it should have been a simple matter, he was fumbling nervously with the magazine.

Chase stood and ran.

He had covered only a third of the distance between them when Judge heard him coming. The man looked up, twisted around the edge of the car and started down the highway, running for all he had.

Still smiling, Chase put his head down, gritted his teeth and made a little more effort. Though he was severely underweight and had not exercised or trained for a year, his muscles responded like well-trained animals. He was gaining on Judge.

The road began to slope as they went over the crest of the rise, then seemed to plummet, so that its angle forced Chase to put less effort into his pursuit lest he pitch forward and lose his balance. Up ahead, a red Volkswagen was parked along the berm, though there was no one to be seen about it. In a moment it was clear that the VW was Judge's car, for he made after it with a renewed burst of speed.

'No!' Chase shouted.

But his voice was weak, nothing more than the soft gasp of dry air escaping from a punctured paper bag, and even he outran the sound of it.

Judge reached the car, flung the door open and piled inside behind the wheel, swinging the door shut after him in one quick, smooth move. He had either left the keys in the ignition or, possibly, had kept the motor running while he went about passing his 'judgment,' for now the Volkswagen pulled away from the edge of the road, screeched as its spinning tyres hit the asphalt and kicked thick smoke out from under them like clouds of white dusting powder. In this one instance, at least, Judge had prepared the way far better than any amateur might be expected to.

Chase did not even have the opportunity to catch part of the licence number, because he was startled out of his wits by the sound of an air horn close behind him, frighteningly close behind.

He threw himself sideways off the road, tripped as the ground dropped under him and rolled over and over on the gravel verge, hugging himself for protection against the stones, until the steep bank brought him to a sudden and somewhat painful stop.

A touch of brakes sounded just once, like the cry of a wounded man. A large moving van – with dark letters against its orange side: U-HAUL – boomed past, moving much too fast on the steep incline of Kanackaway Ridge Road, swaying slightly back and forth as its load shifted. Chase had time to wish that it would catch up with the Volkswagen and plow right over it without slowing down. Then it was out of sight.

Six

There was a two-inch scratch on his forehead, just above his right eye, and a slightly smaller cut on his right cheek, both inflicted by the thorns in the bramble row, both of them already crusted with dried blood. The tips of four fingers were likewise scarred by the brambles, but they were the wounds least to be worried about; in the midst of a dozen other pains, they were unnoticeable. His ribs ached from having rolled for some distance on the gravel berm of the Kanackaway Ridge Road – though none of them seemed broken when he tested them with his hands – and his chest, back and arms were bruised where the largest stones had dug in for a prolonged moment as he passed over them. Both his knees had been skinned open and wept thin blood. He had lost his shirt, of course, when he ripped it in two as protection from the thorns, and his trousers were fit only for the trash can.

CHASE

He sat in the Mustang by the edge of the park, assessing the damage done, and he was not at all relieved, as some might well have been, that he had got away with minor abrasions when he might have lost his life. He was so angry that he wanted to strike out at something, anything, or, failing that, scream at the top of his voice. Over the course of several minutes, however, as he caught his breath and as the sharpness of his pains settled into many small, dull aches, his urge to action was tempered by his common sense. There was nothing to be gained by running off in a rabbit-quick mood of revenge. Sit still. Settle down. Think it out.

Already a few cars had arrived at lovers' lane, driving over the sod to the hedges, where they eagerly took advantage of the first sheets of darkness. The stars were not even out yet, nor the last traces of sunset scoured from the rim of the sky, but the lovers were game. Chase was amazed at their bravura in returning to the scene of the murder while the madman who had knifed Michael Karnes was still on the loose. He wondered if they would lock their car doors tonight.

Since there well might be police patrols along Kanackaway yet, hoping for the killer to make a second attempt, the most suspicious thing would be a man sitting alone in his car. Chase started the motor, raced the engine once or twice, then turned around and started back into the city.

As he drove, he tried to recall everything he had seen so that no clue as to Judge's real identity might slip by. Judge owned a silenced pistol and a red Volkswagen. He was a bad shot, but judging from the way he had taken off, a fairly good driver. Judge got nervous easily, as his blind firing had proved. And that was about the sum of it.

What next? The police?

But when he remembered Wallace and his patronizing tone, he rejected that right away. He had sought help from Cauvel and been given a form of aid he did not want and could not use, advice that was superfluous. The police had been even less help. That left only one thing for it. He would have to handle the whole business himself, open his eyes and ears and begin to track Judge down before Judge killed him.

The decision made, he could not imagine how he had ever contemplated handling the situation any other way.

Mrs Fiedling met him at the door, stepped backwards in surprise when she saw what condition he was in. She put a hand before her mouth and sucked in a breath so nicely that the gesture looked planned. She said, 'What happened to you?'

'I fell down,' Chase said. 'It's nothing.'

'But there's blood on your face,' she said. Chase noted with interest that she hadn't put her hand to her breast in surprise, but to her mouth – and her dress was open the usual three buttons. 'And just look at you, all skinned and bruised!'

'Really, Mrs Fiedling, I'm perfectly all right now. I had a little accident, but I'm on my feet and breathing.'

She looked him over more carefully now, as if she might be getting a bit of a charge from the details of his wounds, and said, 'Have you been drinking again,

Mr Chase?' Her tone had gone swiftly from that of concern to outright disapproval. That was all the more noticeable because this was the first time she had mentioned his fondness for whisky since she had learned that he was a hero.

'No drinks at all,' Chase said.

'You know I don't approve.'

'I know,' he said, starting past her for the stairs. They looked a long way off.

'You didn't wreck your car?' she called after him.

'No,' he said.

He started up the steps, looking anxiously ahead toward the turn at the landing which signified escape of sorts. Strangely, though, he did not feel nearly as oppressed by Mrs Fiedling as he did most times he encountered her.

'That's good news,' she said. 'As long as you have your car, you'll be able to look for jobs much better than before.' Her blue fur mules slapped on the hall floor as she walked toward the steps.

'That's right!' he called back to her.

He turned the landing, steadying himself with a hand on the polished rail. From that point, he took the steps two at a time, even though his legs protested, walked briskly down the second-floor corridor and climbed the attic steps to his own apartment. In his room, he bolted the door and relaxed.

After he had taken in a glass of Jack Daniel's over ice, he drew a tub of water as hot as he could tolerate it, and settled into it much like an old man with arthritis or worse complaints. It slopped over his open sores and made him sigh both with pleasure and pain in equal measure. It was almost as if the water were pouring *through* him.

Forty-five minutes later, clean, he dressed his worst wounds with Merthiolate and put on lightweight slacks, a sports shirt, socks and loafers. With a second glass of whisky in hand, he sat down in the easy chair to contemplate his next move. He looked forward to action with a mixture of excitement and apprehension.

The most natural course seemed to be to speak with Louise Allenby, the girl who had been with Michael Karnes the night he was killed. They had been questioned separately by the police, but there was always the possibility they might be able to come up with something that one or both of them had overlooked that night – especially if they worked together, feeding each other bits of memories to see if anything sparked.

The telephone book listed eighteen Allenbys in the city, but the problem was not as complex as all that, for Chase remembered Louise telling Detective Wallace that her father was dead and her mother had not remarried. Only one of the Allenbys in the book was listed as a woman: Cleta Allenby on Pine Street, an address in the Ashside district.

He dialled the number and waited through ten rings before it was answered. The voice on the other end, though less affected by fear now, was clearly the voice of Louise Allenby. There was a languor to it, more of a throaty womanliness than he had remembered or would have imagined. She answered by giving her name.

'This is Mr Chase, Louise,' he said. 'Do you remember me?'

'Of course,' she said. She sounded genuinely pleased to hear from him, but then perhaps anyone is pleased to talk to someone who saved her life. She said, 'How are you?'

'Fine,' he said, nodding as if she were able to see him. Then he checked himself and said, 'Well, really, not so fine at all.'

'What is it?' she asked, her voice concerned now. 'Is there anything I can do to help?'

'I'd like to talk to you, if possible,' Chase said. 'About what happened Monday night.'

'Well – sure, all right,' she said.

'It won't upset you?'

'No,' she said. And from the note of flippancy in her voice, he knew that was the truth. She said, 'Can you come over now?'

'If it's convenient, I'd very much like to,' he said.

'Fine. It's ten o'clock now – in half an hour, at ten-thirty? Will that be all right?'

'Just right,' Chase said.

'I'll be expecting you.'

She put the phone down so gently that for several long seconds Chase did not realize she had hung up.

His bruises were beginning to stiffen him, so that he felt bound by a length of flat, waxed cord. He stood up and stretched, found his car keys and quickly finished his drink.

When it was time to go, he did not want to begin. Suddenly he realized how completely this one act, this assumption of responsibility, would destroy the simple routines by which he had survived in the months since his discharge from both the army and the hospital. There would be no more leisurely mornings in town, no more afternoons watching old movies on television, no more evenings reading and drinking until he could sleep – at least not for a long while, not until this entire mess was straightened out, from the apprehension of Judge through the trial and its aftermath. Yet, if he remained here, in his own room, if he took his chances, he might remain alive until Judge was caught in a few weeks or, at most, a few months.

Then again, Judge might not miss the next time.

He cursed everyone who had forced him out of his comfortable niche – Zacharia, the local press, the Merchants' Association, Judge, Dr Cauvel, Wallace, Tuppinger – but he knew that he had no choice but to get on with it. His only consolation was the certainty that their victory was only a temporary one. When this was all finished with, he would come back to his room and close the door and reorganize his routines, again settle into the quiet and unchallenging life he had established for himself during the past year.

Mrs Fiedling did not bother him on his way out of the house, and he chose to see this as a good omen.

The Allenbys, mother and daughter, lived in a two-storey neo-Colonial brick home on a small lot in the middle-income-bracket section of Ashside. Two Dutch elm trees were featured at the head of the short flagstone walk and two tiny pine trees at the end of it. Two steps rose to a white door with a brass knocker. The knocker, when lifted and let fall, not only produced a hollow *tok,* but activated door chimes as well, a touch which Chase found unpleasant in the same way he found gilt-edged mirrors, souvenir ashtrays and brightly coloured afghans distasteful.

Louise answered the door herself. She was wearing white shorts and a thin white halter top, and she looked as if she had spent the last half-hour putting on her make-up and brushing her long hair. 'Come in,' she said, stepping aside to give him room.

The living room was what he had expected: expensive Colonial furniture, a colour television set in an enormous and wasteful console cabinet, knotted rugs over polished pine floors – and just the hint of carelessness in the way the house was kept: magazines spilling out of their rack, dried water rings on the coffee table and a trace of dust on the lower rungs of the spindly chairs.

'Sit down,' Louise said. 'The sofa's comfortable, and so's that big chair with the flowered print. The rest of them are like cafeteria chairs at school. Mother's crazy about antiques and Colonial styles. I hate all that kind of stuff.'

He smiled and chose the sofa. 'I'm sorry to bother you like this, so late at night –'

'Don't worry about that,' she said, interrupting in a breezy and very self-confident manner. Indeed, he hardly recognized her as the girl he had taken, whimpering, from Michael Karnes's car on Monday night. 'Since I'm finished with school, I only go to bed when I feel like it, usually around three or three-thirty in the morning.' She smiled abruptly, changing the subject with her expression. 'May I get you a drink?'

'No, thanks,' Chase said.

'Mind if I have something?'

'Go ahead,' he said.

He watched her trim legs scissor as she went to the

pull-down bar shelf concealed in the wall bookcase. As she took out the ingredients for a Sicilian Stinger, she stood with her back to him, her hips artfully canted, her round ass thrust toward him. It might have been the unconscious stance of a girl with all the attributes of a woman but with only a partial understanding of the effect her pneumatic body might have on men. Or it might have been completely contrived.

When she came back with what appeared to be a professionally mixed drink, he said, 'Are you old enough to drink?'

'Seventeen,' she said. 'Almost eighteen, out of high school, starting college in the fall, no longer a child.'

'Of course,' he said, feeling stupid. He'd heard her tell this to the detective. What in the world was the matter with him, reacting to her as if he were a parent himself? There was little more than seven years between them, after all, not nearly enough time to permit him to question her codes. It was just that only seven years ago, when he was her age, one *was* a child at seventeen. Again he had forgotten how fast they grew up now – or how fast they thought they did.

'Sure you won't have something?' she asked, sipping at the drink.

He declined again.

She leaned back against the couch, crossing her bare legs, and she made him aware for the first time that he could see the hard tips of her small breasts against the thin halter.

He said, 'It's just occurred to me that your mother may have been in bed, if she gets up early for work. I didn't mean –'

'Mother's working now,' Louise said. She looked at

him coyly. Or perhaps she didn't realize the effect of the look, with her lashes lowered and her head tilted to one side. 'She's a cocktail waitress. She goes on duty at seven, off at three, home about three-thirty in the morning.'

'I see.'

'Are you frightened?' she asked, smiling now. 'Of being here alone with me?'

'Of course not,' he said, smiling, leaning back on the sofa, turning sideways to see her. But he knew now that none of her sensuality was unintentional.

'Well,' she said, 'where do we begin?' She made a distinct try for the double entendre.

Chase ignored that, and for the following half-hour, guided her through her memories of Monday night, augmenting them with his own, questioning her on details and urging her to question him, looking for some small thing that might be the key or for some change of perspective that might put the madness in a more orderly light. Though they came up with nothing new and though they had little hope, she answered all his questions with a genuine effort to dissect the events of that night. She looked upon them almost as a disinterested outsider, and she appeared to have to make little effort to achieve this tone, as if they really were little more than second-hand stories already.

'Mind if I have another one?' she asked, shaking her glass.

'Go ahead.'

'Want one this time?'

'No, thank you,' he said, recognizing the need to keep his head clear, though not the reason.

CHASE

She stood mixing her drink in the same provocative pose as before, and when she returned to the couch, she sat down much closer to him than she had been before. 'One thing I just thought of,' she said.

'What's that?'

'You asked me if he was wearing a ring, and I said he was. But I forgot to say how he was wearing it.'

Chase leaned away from the back of the couch, eager for anything, no matter how unimportant it seemed at the moment. 'I don't understand what you mean,' he said.

'It was a pinkie ring,' she said.

'A what?'

She wiggled the smallest finger on her free hand. 'A pinkie ring, for your pinkie, your littlest finger. Haven't you ever seen one?'

'Of course,' he admitted. 'But I really don't understand where it tells us anything new or important.'

'Well,' she said, making a face that seemed divorced from any possible human emotion, '*I've* only seen them on girls – or on fairies.'

He considered that for a moment and decided that they might be onto something after all. 'Then you think the killer might be a – homosexual?'

'I don't know,' she said. 'But it *was* a pinkie ring.'

'Did you tell Wallace about this?'

'I just now thought of it. You loosened me up, and it just came back to me in a flash.'

He liked that. He could not think of anything more personally gratifying than slowly establishing a body of information about Judge – working outward from this first essential bit of data – and then presenting it to

88

the police with just the proper note of disdain after they had written him off as a borderline mental case with complex delusions. If that was childish, so be it. A long time had passed since he had indulged himself in anything childish.

'It may be a help,' he said.

She slid next to him with all the oiled smoothness of a machine made especially for seduction, all soft lines and golden tan. 'Do you think so, Mr Chase?'

He nodded, trying to decide how best to excuse himself without hurting her feelings. He could feel her thigh pressuring his.

She put her drink down and looked at him sideways, though she made certain that he saw her glance.

He stood up abruptly and said, 'I ought to be going. This has given me something concrete to consider, more than I had hoped for.' That was only a small lie, since he'd really not expected anything.

She stood up too, very close to him. 'Oh, it's early,' she said. 'I wish you'd stay and keep me company.'

Close to her, he could smell the combination of womanly scents – perfume, soap, freshly washed hair, the hint of sex – that usually intrigued a man, but he was not the least bit intrigued. Aroused, yes. Amazingly aroused over a woman for the first time in many months. But arousal was something separate from intrigue. Though she was lithe and quite lovely, he could not seem to want her to any extent further than his erection, never a particularly reliable device for measuring the quality of any relationship between a man and a woman.

'No,' he said. 'I've other people to see.'

'At this hour?'

'One or two other people,' he insisted, aware that he was losing the initiative.

She moved against him, leaned up and licked his lips. No kiss. Just the maddeningly quick flicking of her pink tongue.

Then he knew why he couldn't let his erection guide him. Though Louise looked like a woman and proceeded like a woman, she was something far less. Not a child, surely, and not a girl. But she lacked a roughened surface, the burnish of contact with life and the problems of life. She had always been protected, and the result was a sensuous polish that would take them both the whole way in one sleek, gliding explosion of sensation – but leave him feeling hollow and bitter afterward. What on earth would they talk about once he had fucked her?

'We've got the house for several hours yet,' she said. 'We don't even have to use the couch. I've got a great big white bed with a white canopy and gold-ringed posts.'

'I can't,' he said. 'I really can't, because these people are waiting for me.'

She was enough of a woman to know when she had lost a point. She stepped back and smiled at him. 'But I do want to thank you. For saving my life. That's something that deserves a big reward.'

'You don't owe me anything,' he said.

'I *do*. Some other night, when you don't have plans?'

Because there was nothing to be gained from angering her, and because he might require her cooperation later, he leaned to her and kissed her on the lips. He said, 'Definitely some other night.'

'That's fine,' she said. 'I know we'll be good together.'

All polish, fast and easy, no jagged edges to get hung up on. Chase wondered if, afterward, her lovers could remember whom they'd been inside of.

He said, 'If Detective Wallace questions you again, do you think you could sort of – forget about the ring?'

She said that she could. 'But why are you carrying on with this on your own? I never did ask.'

'Personal,' he said. 'For personal reasons.'

At home again, he thought about what he had learned, and he was no longer sure that it was at all important. The fact that Judge wore a pinkie ring was not conclusive proof of any sexual aberration – just as long hair was no proof of revolutionary tendencies and violent desires, as a skimpy miniskirt in no way indicated that the girl wearing it was available because she showed a lot of leg. And even if Judge were a homosexual, his hang-up did not make him particularly more easy to find. Of course, there were places in the city where the gay crowd congregated, and Chase knew most of them, if they had not gone out of fashion. But there were bound to be hundreds at such watering spots – with no guarantee that Judge would be found frequenting such places. As with every sexual minority in America, there were ten closet queens for every liberated man who stepped forward to be counted.

He undressed, feeling gloomy again, and got a glass from the cupboard. He carried it to the refrigerator and put two ice cubes in it, but when he picked up the whisky bottle, he realized he did not need another drink to get to sleep. He crawled beneath the covers, bone-weary, leaving the ice to melt, reached over and turned out the bedside lamp. The darkness was heavy and warm and, for the first time in longer than he could remember, comforting.

Alone now, on the edge of sleep, he began to wonder if he had been a fool not to respond to Louise Allenby's blatant sexual offerings. He had been months without a woman and without a desire for one. She had been game and, in the physical department anyway, she would most likely have been perfect, sure and thrilling in her movements. Why had he thought there must be more than a swift coupling, an orgasm?

Had he retreated from the prospect because he feared it would draw him even further into the world, further away from his precious routines than ever? A relationship with a woman, no matter how transitory, would definitely be an admission of one more break-down in his carefully mortared walls.

He turned and burrowed into the pillow, for he did not want to think about that any longer. However, he had no choice; the thoughts came unbidden. And, shortly, he had a realization whose import he could not immediately assess, not even to the extent of assigning it a positive or negative value. He had rejected Louise Allenby to preserve his sexual routine – but had immediately afterward broken an equally important ritual that was an integral part of his hermit's existence, his penitence: he had foregone his glass of whisky.

Seven

For a split second when he woke the following morning, he thought he was suffering from the grandfather of all hangovers, and then he realized it was only the aftereffect of the falls he had taken Thursday evening. Each contusion and laceration seemed to have swelled and grown darker, filled up with pain so pure that he felt he ought to be able to squeeze it out in a steady stream of liquid the colour of, say, fine brandy. His eyes felt sunken and served as twin focuses for a headache that ranged all over his scalp. When he sat up and tried to get out of bed, his muscles protested like rusted bands of steel working against each other without benefit of lubrication.

He felt so bad, in fact, that he was not even frightened by the usual array of nightmares, dismissing them in order to pay more elaborate attention to the ache that was everywhere in him.

In the bathroom, his hands gripping the sink as he

leaned toward the spotted mirror, he saw that his face was drawn and much paler than it should have been, dark rings nesting under his eyes. His chest and back were dotted with bruises, most of them about as large as a thumbprint and painful out of all proportion to their size.

He convinced himself that a hot bath would soothe him, but he found it only made things worse. Back in the main room, he began to walk and to swing his arms, biting down on the pain as if he might be able to kill it if he didn't give voice to it. He forced himself through a dozen push-ups and countless deep-knee bends until he was dizzy and felt as if he might faint. Where the bath had failed, the exercises helped, though only to a minute degree. He knew the only cure was activity, and he dressed to begin the day.

In the light of the day, with his pain about him like a cloak, he thought his plan was stupid and doomed to failure from the moment of conception, but he also knew that he could not yet stop his investigation. He was still driven by a combination of fear and the desire to prove himself to Cauvel, Wallace and the rest of them. Until one or the other of those motivations disappeared, the mix was an effective spur to keep him going. Taking each step like an octogenarian, he went downstairs.

'Mail for you,' Mrs Fiedling said, slapping her mules as she shuffled out from the living room. She picked up a plain brown envelope from the pine table in the hall and handed it to him. She said, 'As you can see, there isn't any return address.'

'Probably advertisements,' Chase said. He took a step toward the front door, hoping that she would not notice his stiffness and inquire about his health.

He need not have worried, for she was more interested in the contents of the envelope than in him. 'It can't be ads in a plain envelope. The only things that come in plain envelopes without return addresses are wedding invitations – of which that doesn't look like one – and dirty literature.' She looked at him and said, 'I won't tolerate dirty literature in my house.'

'And I don't blame you,' Chase said.

'Then it isn't?'

'No,' he said, slitting it open with his finger and withdrawing the Xeroxed psychiatric file and journal articles. 'A friend of mine who knows my interest in psychology and psychiatry sends me interesting articles on the subject when he find them.'

'Oh,' Mrs Fiedling said, obviously surprised that Chase harboured such intellectual and hitherto unknown interests. 'Well, I hope I didn't embarrass you, but I couldn't tolerate having pornography in my home.'

Chase only barely refrained from commenting on her unbuttoned dress. 'I understand,' he said. 'Now, if you'll excuse me, I have to be going.'

'Job interview?' she asked.

'Yes.'

'Then I won't be the one to hold you up!'

He went out to his car and sank into the bucket seat behind the wheel, taking a moment to draw several deep breaths of fresh air. He started the car and drove far enough down the street to be out of sight of the house, kerbed, let the engine idle as he examined the Xeroxed pages which Judge had sent him.

If he had hoped to find something in these papers to

further convince him that his present attitudes were foolish and that he should go back to his room and forget the private investigation he had begun, he was disappointed. Instead, Cauvel's records engendered even a greater stubbornness, a more fierce anger and a stronger desire to prove himself. The pages of handwritten notes that had been made during their sessions were so difficult to read that he passed over them for the time being, but he studied the three published and two as yet unpublished articles that concerned him. In all of them, Cauvel's high self-esteem was evident, and his egotism had subtly distorted everything which he had reported to his colleagues. Though he never used Chase's real name, Chase knew himself in the articles – but as if he were looking at himself and the history of his mental condition through a curiously distorting glass. Every annoying symptom he suffered had been exaggerated to make their eventual amelioration seem more of an achievement on Cauvel's part. All the clumsy probes that Cauvel had initiated went unmentioned while he claimed credit for techniques he had never employed but had apparently developed through hindsight. And when Cauvel referred to him, it was with an unfair summation of the man-boy he had been before Nam, with a disdain completely unjustified. It was this, in the end, that brought Chase's growing irritation to a burst of anger: he jammed the sheets back into the envelope, put the Mustang in gear and drove away from there, more intent on amassing a body of information about Judge than he had ever been.

The Metropolitan Bureau of Vital Statistics, in the

basement of the courthouse, was a model of efficiency. The office itself, fronting the long, well-lighted data storage vaults, was small and neat, containing four filing cabinets, three typewriters, a copying machine, a long worktable, a tiny refrigerator-hotplate combination, two huge square desks with matching, sturdy chairs – and two equally study elderly women who banged away at their typewriters with a rhythmic swiftness that seemed almost arranged and conducted. The only open space was a railed foyer inside the door and aisles that led directly from each desk to each piece of essential equipment. Chase stood in the foyer and cleared his throat, though he was sure they had both seen him come in. The stoutest of the two women typed to the end of the page, pulled the form out of the carriage and placed it neatly in a box full of similar forms. She looked up at Chase then, and she smiled. It was an efficient smile, showing just enough teeth and turning up just far enough at the corners to be identifiable in any catalogue of human expressions. When she had held it a second or two, long enough to convey a minimum of professional courtesy and friendliness, she let it go. Her lips settled into a straight line which was neither smile nor frown but which, Chase supposed, saved a good deal of energy and kept her face as relatively free of age lines as it was.

She said, 'May I help you?'

He had already decided on the tack that Judge most likely had used when he had come here researching Chase's life. He said, 'I'm doing a family history, and I was wondering if I could be permitted to look up a few things in the city records.'

'Certainly,' the stout woman said, rising from her seat in one quick movement. The name on her deskplate was MRS ONUFER; her workmate, MRS KLOU, had not even looked up but was still battling away at her keyboard.

Mrs Onufer came around her desk, passed the gate in the railing and motioned him to follow her. She led him to the rear of the room, through a fire door and into a large concrete-walled chamber that was ringed with filing cabinets and lined with others in ten neat parallel rows in the middle of the floor. There was a worktable with three chairs at it, the table scarred and the chairs all unpadded.

'You'll see stickers on the cabinets that tell you what's inside – that section to the right is birth certificates, the one further down being bar and restaurant licences, then health department records. Against the far wall are the selective service carbons which we keep for a nominal yearly rental, beside those are the minutes and budets of City Council going back thirty-seven years. You get the idea. Each drawer is labelled according to one of two filing systems, depending on the nature of the material, either alphabetically or by date. Whatever you remove from the files must be left on this table to be returned to its proper place later. Do not attempt to replace what you pull from the files; that is my job, and I do it far more accurately than you would.' Here she flashed a quick, economical smile. 'You may not take anything from this room. For a nominal fee, Mrs Klou will provide copies of whatever documents interest you. If anything should be removed from this room, you will be subjected to a possible fine of five thousand dollars and two years in prison.'

'Thank you for your help,' Chase said.

'And no smoking,' she said.

'Of course not.'

She turned and walked out of the room, closing the door behind her, her tapping heels swiftly fading until he could hear nothing but his own lungs drawing in breath after breath.

It had been that simple for Judge. Chase had hoped, irrationally, that there was some procedure whereby those who used these files were identified. Now he saw that Mrs Onufer would not be bothered with such a time-consuming routine, for she could be more than certain that no one would slip by her with stolen papers under his coat. She would notice the look of guilt as swiftly as a nasty dog notices fear in the face of a potential opponent.

He looked up his own birth certificate, found the minutes of the council meeting in which the city fathers had voted an award in his honour. In the carbons of the selective service records, he found the pertinent facts concerning his own eligibility history, with only the confidential correspondence removed. When he felt he had passed enough time to keep from arousing Mrs Onufer's suspicions, he left the storage vaults.

'Find what you were looking for?' Mrs Onufer asked.

'Yes, thank you.'

'No trouble, Mr Chase,' she said, turning back to her work.

That stopped him. He said, 'You know me?'

She looked up, flashed a smile just a fraction of a

second longer than her business smile and said, 'I read the papers every evening.'

Instead of walking to the door, he crossed to her desk. 'If you had not known me,' he said, 'would you have asked for a name before I went in there to root around?'

'Why, of course,' she said. 'No one has ever taken any records in the twelve years I've been here, but I still see the need for some safety check.'

'And you keep a list?'

She tapped a notebook on the edge of her desk. 'I just put your name down, out of habit.'

He said, 'This may sound like an odd request, but could you tell me who was here this past Tuesday?'

She looked at him, looked at the book, reached a quick decision. 'I don't see why I should hesitate,' she said. 'There's nothing confidential in the list.' She opened it, thumbed through several pages, then said, 'Only three people all day.' She showed him the names.

When he had them well in mind, he said, 'Thank you. You see, I'm constantly being bothered by reporters who want stories, and I don't care for all the publicity. I think they've said everything about me there is to be said. But I've heard there's a local man working up a series for a national magazine, against my wishes, and I wondered if he'd been here Tuesday as I'd been told.'

Even he thought the lie sounded utterly absurd, and he had no hope of her believing him, until he realized that he would not have had to offer her any explanation whatsoever. She trusted him. Everyone trusted a hero. She nodded at his fabrication as if it were perfectly logical, and she commiserated – for a few brief moments – on the problems of unwanted publicity he must have to face. Then, conscious of the time she had been wasting, she bent her head to her work and thereby dismissed him.

When he left the office, he realized that Mrs Klou had never once looked up and had not paused even for a moment in the furious pace she set at the typewriter.

It was a quarter to twelve when he stepped out of the courthouse, and he was surprisingly hungry. He got his Mustang out of the lot after paying a dollar ransom to the man in the ticket booth, then drove out Galasio Boulevard to the string of drive-in eateries that had sprung up like glass-and-aluminium mushrooms since he had gone away to war. He parked in a slot at the Diamond Dell and ordered more food than he thought he could eat. A cute redhead in tight hotpants brought his food, accepted his money and said she hoped he'd like everything. By a quarter to one he had consumed everything on the tray, more than he had eaten in any three meals during the last year.

At a nearby gas station, he used the telephone booth directory to find numbers for two of the three people who had browsed through city files on Tuesday, and called them. Both were women, rather elderly, and both did exist. The third name, Howard Devore, was a phony. It did not appear in the telephone book, and when he looked later, was not in the city directory. The man might be from out of town, of course. But Chase didn't think that was the answer. Howard Devore, he felt certain, was an alias that Judge had used.

CHASE

Because he did not trust himself to store his knowledge logically and to notice links between bits of diverse data, Chase purchased a small ring-bound notebook and an inexpensive plastic pen, and he carefully listed the following:

1. Alias – Judge
2. Alias – Howard Devore
3. Possible homosexual
4. No criminal record, prints not on file
5. Has knowledge of lock-picking, broke into Cauvel's office
6. Owns a red Volkswagen
7. Owns a silenced pistol, probably a .32 calibre

Chase looked over the list when he was finished with it, thought a moment, then added an eighth fact, one which struck him, somehow, as important: '8. May be either unemployed, on vacation or on a leave of absence.' That seemed the only way to explain how he had been able to call Chase at any hour of the day, follow him in the middle of the afternoon and waste two days 'researching' Chase's life. He neither sounded nor acted old enough to be retired. Unemployed, then. Or on a vacation. If the former were the case, his field of suspects could be drastically narrowed, though the resultant group would still be quite large. If it were the latter, and if Judge were on vacation, the number of hours a day that Chase was endangered would be reduced in a week or two when Judge was back on the job.

He closed the notebook and started the car, aware that the last thought had been a dangerous slipping back, wishful thinking that could do nothing more than weaken his resolve.

The girl who was in charge of the *Press-Dispatch* morgue room was only two inches under six feet, and nearly six in her low heels, almost as tall as Chase, with yellow hair to the middle of her back, a skirt to the middle of her thighs, and legs that just went on forever. Her name was Glenda Kleaver, and she spoke with an anachronistically small, soft, feminine voice that was yet strangely at home in her fine, big body.

She demonstrated the use of microfilm viewers to Chase and explained that all editions prior to January 1, 1966, were now stored on film to conserve space. She explained the procedure for ordering the proper spools and for obtaining the mint editions that had not yet been transferred to film.

Several reporters were sitting at the machines, twisting the control knobs and staring into the viewers, jotting on note pads beside them.

Chase said, 'Do you get many outsiders here?'

The girl smiled at him, and he decided she could not be more than nineteen or twenty, though she had that burnish of life which Louise Allenby lacked. She leaned back against the edge of her desk, crossing her slim legs, fished a cigarette from a pack on the desk and lighted it. She said, 'I'm trying to quit these things, so don't be surprised if I only hold it and don't smoke it.' She crossed her arms under her large breasts and said, 'A newspaper morgue is chiefly for the use of the staff and for the police. But we keep it open to the public without charge. We get maybe a dozen people a week.'

'What are they looking for here?'

'What are *you* looking for?' she asked.

He hesitated only a moment, then gave her the same story he had first given Mrs Onufer at the Metropolitan Bureau of Vital Statistics. He said, 'I'm gathering facts for a family history.'

Glenda Kleaver nodded, raised the cigarette to her lips, then put it down without drawing on it. She said, 'That's what most outsiders come here for. You'd be surprised how many people are tracking down their ancestors with an idea of immortalizing them.'

There was a distinct note of sarcasm in her voice, and he felt that he had to justify the lie he'd told her. 'I don't want to immortalize anyone,' he said. 'My family history will go unwritten.'

'Just curiosity, then?' she asked. She picked up her cigarette from the ashtray and held it.

'Yes,' he said.

'I haven't the least bit of curiosity about dead relatives. I don't even like the living relatives very much.'

He laughed. 'No sense of pride in your name, your lineage?'

'None. It's probably more mutt than thoroughbred, anyway.' She put her cigarette down now, her slim fingers holding it like a precise surgical instrument.

Chase would have liked to go on talking about anything but Judge, because he felt terribly at ease with her, more at ease than he had felt in the presence of a woman since . . . Since Jules Verne, the underground operation in Nam. But he recognized his urge to be garrulous as a further evasion of the issue at hand. He said, 'So I don't have to sign anything to use the files?'

'No,' she said. 'I have to get everything for you, and you have to return it to me before you leave.'

He tried to think of some way he could ask her about any outsiders who had used the morgue this past Tuesday, but no convenient cover story came to mind. He could not employ the same device he had used with Mrs Onufer, the tale of the nosy reporter, for he would not find any sympathy with that routine, not here of all places. If he told her the truth or a portion of the truth, she might or might not believe him, and if she did not, he would feel like a prize ass. Oddly enough, though he had only just met her, he did not want to be embarrassed in front of her. In the end, he could say nothing.

Besides, another ugly possibility had occurred to him. There were two reporters in the room just then, and one of them was quite likely to learn who he was and what he was doing there if he said anything to the girl. He could not escape, then, seeing his picture on the front page and reading all about this latest development in his life. They might treat the story either straight or tongue-in-cheek (probably the latter if they talked to the police and then to Cauvel), but either way it would be an intolerable development.

'Now,' Glenda said, 'what would you like to have first?'

Before he could respond, one of the reporters at the microfilm machines looked up from his work and said, 'Glenda, could I have all the dailies between May 15, 1952, and September 15 of that same year?'

'In a moment,' she said, grinding out her unsmoked cigarette. 'This gentleman was first.'

'That's okay,' Chase said, grasping the opportunity. 'I've got plenty of time.'

'You sure?' she asked.

'Yeah. Get him what he needs.'

'I'll be back in five minutes,' she said.

As she walked the length of the small room and through the wide arch into the filing room, both Chase and the reporter watched her. She was tall but not clumsy, moving with a sensuous, feline grace that actually made her seem fragile.

When she had gone, the reporter said, 'Thanks for waiting.'

'That's okay.'

'I've got an eleven o'clock deadline on this piece, and I haven't even begun to get my sources together.' He turned back to his viewer and scanned the last article, so engrossed in his work that he had not, apparently, recognized Chase.

Chase used the opportunity to leave the room. He had been afraid, before the fortunate interruption, that he was going to have to request materials and waste an hour or more going through them in order to play out the role he had established for himself.

Back in his Mustang, he opened his notebook and looked at the list, but he had absolutely nothing to add to it, and he could not see any pertinent connections between the familiar eight items. He closed the book, started the car and drove out into the traffic on John F. Kennedy Throughway.

Fifteen minutes later he was on the four-lane interstate beyond city limits, the speedometer steady at seventy miles an hour, wind whistling at the open windows and rustling through his hair. As he drove, he thought about Glenda Kleaver, and he hardly noticed the miles going by.

After high school Chase had gone to State because it was just over forty miles from home and, therefore, offered several advantages not to be had at more distant universities. For one thing, his mother was pleased that he could come home more often than at Christmas and spring holidays, though that was only a minor sales point to Chase. He was sold on State because it meant he could still use his father's completely equipped garage for an engine tune-up for his Dodge every month. He had inherited his love of automobiles from his father and would have experienced a deal of anxiety at being long away from proper mechanic facilities. (In the war, when all machines came to mean something totally different to Chase, he lose his enthusiasm for such tinkering.) Also, being so close to home, he could continue to maintain contact with the girls he had dated who were a year or two years behind him in high school. If he should find the girls at State too sophisticated to pay him much mind, he knew there were several still-willing young ladies at home, easily accessible, every weekend if he needed them that often. (In the war, Chase had been bleached of his male chauvinism, though that had been replaced with something far worse – with a complete lack of interest, a boredom so profound that even he was disturbed by it.)

Now, as he parked before the administration building, he felt like a stranger to the place, as if he had not spent nearly four years of his life in and about these buildings, on these flagstone paths and under the rich canopies of willows and elms. That part of his life had been divorced from this moment by the war, and to recapture the essence of those memories and moods would entail crossing again through the stream of the war to the shores of the past, an act he could not indulge in simply for the sake of sentimentality. He was a stranger to this place, then, and would remain so.

He found the Student Records Office where it had been for fifty-odd years, and he recognized most of the people who worked there, though he had never known any of their names. This time, when he was approached by the office manager, he decided that the simple truth was the best key to a proper response. He gave his name and sketchily explained his purpose.

'I should have recognized you, but I didn't,' the manager said. He was a small, pale, nervous man who wore a neatly clipped moustache and an old-fashioned, floppy-collared white dress shirt. He kept picking things up and putting them down to no end. His name was Brown, and he said he was pleased to meet such a distinguished alumnus. 'But there have been dozens of requests for your files in recent months, ever since the medal was announced. You must have been contacted for a number of excellent jobs.'

Chase ignored the indirect question. He said, 'Do you keep names and addresses of people requesting records?'

'Of course!' Brown said. 'We only give information to businessmen.'

'Fine,' Chase said. 'Then I'm looking for the man

who came in on a Tuesday, this past Tuesday.'

'Just a moment,' Brown said. He fetched a ledger and brought it to the counter, put it down, then picked it up again and thumbed through it. 'There was just one gentleman,' he said.

'Who was he?'

Brown showed Chase the address as he read it. 'Eric Blentz, Gateway Mall Tavern. It's in the city.'

'I know where it's at,' Chase said.

'Has he offered you a position?'

'No.'

'But I thought you said he was bothering you,' Brown said. He picked up a fountain pen lying on the counter, twisted it in his fingers and put it down again.

'He is, but not to take a job with him.'

Brown looked at the ledger, still not comprehending that anyone would use privileged information for anything but what it was meant for. 'If I were you, Mr Chase, I wouldn't accept anything he offered, no matter what the salary.'

'Oh?'

'I don't believe he'd be a pleasant man to work for.'

'You remember him, then?'

Brown lifted the pen again, replaced it. 'Naturally,' he said. 'We do most of our work by mail. It isn't often that a prospective employer comes here for a report.'

'Do you remember what Blentz looked like?'

'Certainly,' Brown said. 'Nearly your height, though not robust at all, very thin, in fact, and with a stoop to his shoulders.'

'How old?'

'Thirty-eight, thirty-nine?'

'His face? Do you remember that?'

'Very ascetic features,' Brown said. 'Very quick eyes. He kept looking from one of my girls to the other, then at me, as if he didn't trust us. His cheeks were rather drawn, and he had an unhealthy complexion. A large but not Mediterranean nose, a thin nose, in fact, so thin that the nostrils were like extended ovals.'

'Brown hair?'

'Blond,' the manager said.

'You said he wouldn't be very pleasant to work for. Why do you think that?'

Brown said, 'He was quite sharp with me, and he didn't look like he could be pleasant if he tried. He was always scowling. He was dressed very neatly, with a high polish to his shoes. I don't think there was a hair out of place on his head, as if he used spray or something. And when I asked for his name and business address, he took the pen out of my hand, turned the ledger around and wrote it down because, as he said, everyone always spelled his name wrong, and he wanted it right this time.'

'A perfectionist?'

'He seemed to be.'

Chase said, 'How is it that you remember him in such detail?'

Brown smiled and picked up the pen, put it down, toyed with the ledger for a moment. He said, 'Evenings and weekends, and especially during the summer, my wife and I run The Footlight, a legitimate theatre in town. I take a role in most of our productions, and I'm always studying people to build a reference of expressions and mannerisms.'

'You must be very good onstage, by now,' Chase said.

CHASE

Brown blushed slightly. 'Not particularly,' he admitted. 'But that kind of thing gets in your blood. We don't make much money on the theatre, but as long as it breaks even, I can indulge myself a little.'

On his way back to his car, Chase tried to picture Brown on the stage, before an audience, his hands trembling, his face paler than ever, his urge to handle things amplified by the circumstances . . . He thought he knew the chief reason The Footlight didn't show much profit.

In the car, Chase opened his notebook and looked over the list of facts, trying to find something that supported the possibility that Judge was Eric Blentz, the saloon owner. To the contrary, he found several things that appeared to conflict. First of all, didn't a man who owned a liquor licence have to be finger-printed as a matter of course? And a man who owned a thriving business like the Gateway Mall Tavern would hardly be driving a Volkswagen. Of course, he could be all wrong about the first thing. And perhaps the VW was Blentz's second car, or even a rented model.

There was one way to find out for sure. He started the car and drove back toward the city, wondering what sort of reception he would get at the Gateway Mall Tavern. . .

111

Eight

The tavern was a jaded reproduction of a German inn, with low, beamed ceilings and white plaster walls X-ed across with dark wooden supports. The six large windows which faced onto the mall promenade were leaded glass the colour of burgundy and only slightly translucent. Around the walls were large, darkly upholstered booths, some designed for a couple by themselves and some for four patrons. Chase took a seat in one of the smaller booths toward the rear of the place and sat facing the bar and the front entrance.

A cheerful, apple-cheeked blonde in a short brown skirt and low-cut white peasant blouse, breasts like overinflated balloons peeking over the lace top, came over and lighted the lantern on his table, then took his order for a whisky sour and departed, swinging her plump little ass in a most unmaidenly manner.

The bar was not especially busy at six o'clock, since it was priced more for the supper-hour crowd; only seven other patrons shared the place, three couples and a lone woman who sat at the bar. None of the young men fit the description Brown had given Chase, and he disregarded them. The bartender was the only other man in the place, aging and bald, with a pot of a stomach, but quick and expert with the bottles and obviously a favourite with the barmaids.

Blentz might not frequent his own tavern, of course, though he would be an exception to the rule if that were the case. Most saloon keepers like not only to hang around to keep a watchful eye on the till, but to bask in the status of a minor celebrity which they acquire with their most regular customers.

Chase realized that he was tense, leaning away from the back of the booth, his hands on top of the table and curled into hard, angular fists. That was no good. He settled back and forced himself to rest, since it was likely that the wait might last hours. He knew his capacity would permit him to drink for that long or longer, all night if necessary, without suffering a lessening of his perceptions. He had had a good deal of practice, after all.

After the second whisky sour, he asked for a menu and ordered a large meal, surprised at his renewed hunger after having consumed a meal at the drive-in only five or six hours earlier. He was sure his eyes were, as predicted by the proverb, bigger than his stomach. But when the food came, he took it in like a man starved and finished every bite of it.

Five drinks after dinner, shortly after nine o'clock, Chase asked the waitress if Mr Blentz would be in this evening.

She looked across the now crowded room and

pointed at a heavy-set man on a stool at the bar. 'That's him,' she said.

'Are you sure?'

The man was around fifty years of age, weighed well over two hundred pounds and was four or five inches shorter than Brown's description.

'I've worked for him for two years,' the blonde said.

'I was told he was tall and slender. Blond hair, sharp dresser.'

'Maybe twenty years ago he was slender and a sharp dresser,' she said. 'But he couldn't ever have been tall or blond.'

'I guess not,' Chase said. 'I guess I must be looking for another Blentz.' He smiled at the girl, trying not to look down her ample cleavage, and said, 'Could I have the bill, please?'

The bill totalled nearly sixteen dollars for the seven drinks and the filet mignon. Chase handed the barmaid a twenty and told her she could keep the change.

Outside, the parking lot was all but deserted, for the majority of the stores in the mall had closed twenty minutes before. The night air was muggy after the air-conditioned tavern and seemed to settle on the macadam like a blanket.

Chase felt perspiration on his forehead, and he wiped at it absent-mindedly as he walked toward the Mustang, thinking about Eric Blentz. He had stepped around the front fender and was only a few feet from the driver's door when the swelling sound of an engine, close behind, caught his attention. Trained to react first and think a split second later, he did not turn to see what was behind him, but placed his hands on

114

the fender and vaulted onto the hood of the Mustang.

An instant later the left front fender of a red Volkswagen struck the black sports car and scraped noisily along the door, only breaking free with a lurch a foot or two from the rear bumper. Sparks hissed up like fireworks and left behind a faint smell of hot metal and scorched paint. Though the car rocked hard when it was struck, Chase held on by curling his fingers over the edge of the trough that housed the recessed windshield wipers. He felt certain that if he fell off, the Volkswagen would change direction and come back at him.

Twenty feet away, the driver of the other car shifted gears with little finesse.

Chase stood up on the hood of the Mustang and stared after the retreating Volkswagen, trying to see the licence number or at least a portion of it. Even if he had been close enough to read the dark numerals, nothing would have been gained, for Judge had twisted a large piece of burlap sacking over the plate. It waved at Chase, almost as if it had been meant to mock him.

The VW reached the exit lane from the mall lot, jolted against the low, curved kerb so hard it looked as if it might shoot across the sidewalk and strike one of the mercury arc standards at the perimeter of the lawn. Then Judge regained control, accelerated, went through the flashing amber traffic light at the intersection, turned right onto the main highway toward the heart of the city. In another fifteen seconds it passed over the brow of the nearest hill and was out of sight.

Chase looked around to see if anyone had

witnessed the short, violent confrontation, and he saw that he was alone.

He got down from the hood and walked the length of the Mustang, examining the damage. The anterior third of the fender was jammed back toward the cut of the driver's door, though it had not been crushed against the tyre and should not present any major problems. Two other grooves, as deep as the diameter of a pencil, with all or nearly all the paint peeled off in a three-inch swathe between them, ran parallel until they reached the point near the back bumper where the VW had been wrenched away. All of it was body work that could be hammered out, though the bill could easily exceed five hundred dollars.

He didn't care.

Money was the least of his worries.

He opened the driver's door and found that it only protested meekly, sat down behind the wheel, closed the door, opened his notebook and reread his list. His hand trembled when he added the ninth, tenth and eleventh items:

  9. Third alias – Eric Blentz
 10. Given to rash action in the face of previous failures
 11. Driving damaged car, left front fender

Even before Judge had made the latest murder attempt, it had been a rough day all around, and he had not got much of anywhere. He sat in the car, staring at the empty lot, until his hands had stopped shaking. Weary, he drove home, wondering where Judge would be waiting for him the next time and whether he had been using the day to practice with his pistol.

The telephone woke him Saturday morning.

He reached for it, and having placed a hand on the cold, hard plastic, realized who might be calling. Judge hadn't phoned since early Wednesday night – unless he had tried to reach Chase on Friday when he was out – but that was not necessarily indicative of any permanent change in his method of operation.

Chase picked up the phone and said. 'Hello?'

'Ben?'

'Yes?'

'Dr Cauvel here.'

It was the first time he had ever heard the psychiatrist on the phone, and he thought the man sounded too nasal, somewhat silly.

'What do you want?' Chase asked. The name had fully awakened him and had overcome the residue of his nightmares.

'I wondered why you hadn't kept your Friday appointment.'

'I didn't feel like it.'

Cauvel said, 'If it was because I talked to the police so frankly, you must understand that –'

'That's only part of it,' Chase said.

'Should we get together this afternoon and talk about it, all of it?' Cauvel asked, adopting his fatherly tone. Even in that role, his underlying smug superiority came through.

'No,' Chase said.

'When should we, then?'

Chase said, 'I'm not coming in again.'

'But you have to!' Cauvel said.

'I don't believe I do. The psychiatric care was not a condition of my hospital discharge, only a benefit I could avail myself of.'

Cauvel thought a moment, abandoned any thought of using implied threats, and said, 'And you still *can* avail yourself of it, Ben. I'm here, waiting to see you–'

'It's no longer a benefit,' Chase said. He realized that he was beginning to enjoy this. For the first time he had Cauvel on the defensive for more than a brief moment, and the switch in positions had a delightful quality of triumph to it.

'Ben, you *are* angry about what I said to the police. That is the whole thing, isn't it?' He was certain that he had the situation analyzed now, all carefully broken down into neat compartments by his clever reasoning powers.

'Partly,' Chase said. 'But there are two other reasons.'

'What?'

'Your articles, for a start.'

'Articles?' Cauvel asked, playing the idiot either consciously or out of confusion.

'You surely did glorify the treatment you gave me, didn't you? In your piece for *Therapy Journal,* you come off like a Sigmund Freud or even a Jesus Christ.'

'You read my articles?'

'All of them,' Chase said. He had almost said *five* of them before he realized that two of the articles had not yet seen print but were only rough drafts in Cauvel's files.

'How did you know they were concerned with your case? I didn't use any real names.'

'A colleague of yours tipped me off,' Chase lied.

'Of *mine?* A fellow professional?'

'Yes,' Chase said. He thought: That's really not too far off base, though. He was a colleague of yours, in a sense – another madman.

'Look, Ben, I'm sure we can talk about this and reach some sort of understanding –'

'You forgot the third reason,' Chase said. 'I told you there were three reasons why I won't be coming back.'

'Yes?'

'Yes,' Chase said. 'The third reason is the best of the lot, Dr Cauvel. You are an egotist, a sonofabitch and a monumentally petty man. I can't stand to be around you, and I find you disgustingly immature.'

He hung up on Cauvel, convinced that he had begun the day in the best manner imaginable.

Later, he was not so sure of that. He genuinely believed all those things he had said about and to Cauvel, and he actually did find the man disgusting. But making the break with his psychiatrist was, in some way he could not clearly define, more of a definite rejection of his more recent life style than anything else he had done. He told himself that when Judge was located and the police received the conclusive proof that he, Chase, would compile against the killer, he could resume his sheltered existence on the third floor of Mrs Fiedling's house. Now he had decided to cease psychiatric treatment, an admission that he was not the same man he had once been and that the burden of guilt he bore was growing distinctly less heavy. He was a bit disconcerted by that.

To make matters worse, once he had shaved and bathed and exercised some of the stiffness out of himself, he found that he had no leads to follow in his investigation. So far as he could think, he had been everywhere that Judge had been, and yet he had gained nothing for his trouble except a fairly accurate description of the man, something that would do him no concrete good unless he could connect a name with it or could think of a place where the description might be recognized. He could hardly tramp through the entire city asking everyone he met if one of them had seen a man with those particular characteristics. And short of that, he did not see what he was going to do with the long day ahead.

Once he had taken breakfast at a pancake house on Galasio Boulevard, however, he was able to think more clearly and more optimistically. He still had two possible sources, no matter how slim a chance might ride on them. He could return to the Gateway Mall Tavern and talk to the real Eric Blentz to see if the man could put a name to Judge's description. It seemed likely that Judge had not just chosen Blentz's name out of the phone book when he used it with Brown. Perhaps he knew Blentz or even more likely, had once worked for him. And even if Blentz could provide no new lead, Chase could go back to Glenda Kleaver, the girl at the *Press-Dispatch* morgue room, and question her about anyone who had come into her office the previous Tuesday – something he had not done right off, for fear of making a fool of himself or arousing the interest of the reporters in the room.

He began with a call to the newspaper morgue, but he found it was not open for business, as he had suspected might be the case. In the phone book he found a listing under the girl's name and dialled that, received an answer on the fourth ring.

'Hello?' she said.

He had forgotten how tiny and soft and feminine her voice was, so breathless that it almost seemed contrived.

He said, 'Miss Kleaver, you probably don't remember me. I was in your office yesterday. My name's Chase. I had to leave while you were out of the room getting information for one of your reporters.'

'I remember you quite well,' she said.

He said, 'My name's Chase, Benjamin Chase, and I'd like to see you again, today, if that's at all possible.'

She hesitated a minute and said, 'Are you asking for a date?'

He said, 'Yes,' though he had not been aware that such a thought was even part of his motive.

She laughed pleasantly. 'Well, you certainly are business-like about it, aren't you?'

'I guess so,' he said, afraid that she would turn him down – and at the same time frightened that she would accept.

'When were you thinking of?' she asked.

'Well,' he said, 'actually, I was thinking about today. This evening. But now I realize that isn't much notice –'

'It's fine,' she said.

'Really?' His throat was tight and his voice sounded a bit higher than usual.

'Yes,' she said. 'One problem, though.'

'What's that?'

'I was planning fondue for supper, and I cut all the meat and seasoned it. I've got everything set out for the rest of the dishes too.'

'Perhaps we could go somewhere after dinner,' he said.

She said, 'I like to eat late. What I was thinking – could you come here for supper? I've more than enough beef for two.'

'That sounds fine,' he said.

She gave him the complete address and said, 'Dress casually, please. And I'll see you at seven.'

'At seven,' he repeated.

When the connection was broken, he stood in the booth, trembling. In the back of his mind, swelling ever larger, was the memory of Operation Jules Verne, the tunnel, the descent, the terrible darkness, the fear, the grate, the women, the guns and, last of all, the blood. His knees felt very weak and his heart beat much faster than it should have done. When he felt dangerously close to being overcome, he leaned back against the glass of the booth and forced himself to reason it out. Accepting a date with Glenda Kleaver was in no way a rejection of his responsibility in the deaths of those Vietnamese women. A long time had passed, after all, and a great deal of penitence had been suffered. And suffered alone. Besides, this was to be only little more than an innocent business meeting, an attempt to learn more about Judge. If Judge could be swiftly located and disposed of, Chase would be able to return to his former hermetic existence much sooner than he had anticipated. Instead of behaving wrongly, therefore, he was taking the surest move toward an end to his present condition and a return to his former, respectable retreat from a way of life that he felt he no longer deserved.

CHASE

He left the booth.

The day was terribly warm and humid. The back of his shirt stuck to him like Saran Wrap.

Driving to the Gateway Mall Tavern, he almost slammed into the rear of three separate automobiles, distracted by the ugly memories which had for a long time been given vent only in his nightmares. The fear of hurting another motorist in an accident and thereby acquiring an even heavier load of guilt had quickly served to sober him and drive the distracting memories down, beyond the veil of recognition.

At the shopping mall, Chase browsed in the bookstore until shortly after noon, then walked up the carpeted slope of the main promenade to the tavern. The barmaid who waited on him said that Blentz was expected in at two o'clock. Chase sat in a corner booth, watching the door, and nursed his drink while he waited.

It was all for nothing. When Blentz arrived at a quarter to three, wearing a white linen suit and a blue shirt that looked slept-in, he was quite willing to accept a drink from Chase and to talk, but he had never employed anyone who fit Judge's description and could not, offhand, think of a friend or regular customer who might be Chase's man.

'You know how it is,' he said. 'Different people every night. Even the regulars change every six months or so.'

'I guess,' Chase said, unable to hide his disappointment. He finished his drink and got up.

'What do you want him for?' Blentz asked. 'He owe you some money?'

'Just the opposite,' Chase said. 'I owe him.'

'How much?'

'Twenty bucks,' Chase lied. 'You still don't know him?'

'I *said* I didn't.' Blentz turned around on his stool. He said, 'How did you go about borrowing twenty bucks from him without learning his name?'

Chase said, 'We were both drunk. If either of us had been a bit more sober, I wouldn't have forgotten that.'

'And if he'd been sober, maybe he wouldn't have loaned the money,' Blentz said. He laughed at his own joke and picked his drink up from the bar.

'Perhaps,' Chase said.

As he walked across the tavern and out the door into the mall, he knew that Eric Blentz was still twisted away from the bar on his stool and was watching him.

He supposed that Blentz might know someone who matched the description but was simply not going to talk about it until he understood a bit more of the situation. Whatever Blentz's background was prior to his ownership of the tavern, it was not the sort of mundane existence most people had. He was not naive and gullible like everyone else Chase had questioned, and he had a canny sense of the law. However, even if Blentz were concealing something, there was no way for Chase to squeeze the information out of him, for Blentz was a private citizen, and Chase was in no way a licenced authority.

He started the car and drove home.

He was not shot at.

In his room, he turned on the television, watched it for fifteen minutes, turned it off before the programme was finished, opened a paperback book, which he found he could not concentrate on, and spent a good deal of time pacing from one wall to the other.

Instinctively, he stayed away from his window.

At six-thirty Chase left the house to keep his date with Glenda Kleaver. When he unlocked the door of the Mustang, he discovered that Judge had been around and had left a message behind for him. The content of the message was clear, though it was wordless. Judge had taken a knife to the smooth vinyl upholstery of the driver's seat, had slashed it so many times that the white stuffing poured out like foam.

He would have liked to believe that the vandalism was completely unrelated to Judge and that he had merely been the innocent victim of some neighbourhood juvenile delinquent with a batch of unbearable frustrations to work out of his system. You heard about that kind of thing nearly every day, after all. They smashed car windows for nothing more than the sound the safety glass made when it splintered. They broke off radio antennae for fun, let the air out of tyres and then slashed them to pieces, poured sand and sugar in the gas tank. Besides, this was something much more readily explained as the pointless protest of some acned adolescent full of misdirected energy than as the carefully considered act of a grown man. An unrepentant murderer would hardy get any thrill out of destruction of property like this.

Yet he knew it was Judge, despite his unvoiced protestations to the contrary.

The delinquent would have slashed all the seats once he had taken the risk of ruining one of them, and he would surely have carried off the stereo tape deck that lay just under the dash, the favourite booty of the young criminal. The delinquent would never have taken the time to lock the door again before leaving. That had been a touch meant to explain the exact conditions of the situation. This had been Judge's work. He had braved the early evening light to use a coat hangar to pop the lock, had worked over the single seat as thoroughly as he had worked on Michael Karnes, had locked up and gone away, sure that his identity and intent would be plainly understood. The car, Judge somehow seemed to realize, was an extension of the man, the modern voodoo doll.

Chase stepped away from the Mustang and looked quickly around to see if he was being watched. It had occurred to him that Judge might be lingering somewhere on the block, interested in the effect of his latest threat. The street, lined with richly leafed elms, closely packed houses and parked cars, afforded an almost infinite number of hiding places, especially in the lengthening shadows of early evening. As carefully as he looked, however, he could not see anyone nearby nor get a glimpse of the red Volkswagen parked along the kerb, and he decided that he was really alone.

It also seemed reasonable to assume that someone had seen Judge force his way into the locked car. When he looked from porch to porch, however, he discovered that no one was out watching the traffic, as was usually the case. Everyone, it appeared, was still inside finishing supper and washing dishes.

He went into the house again, without encountering Mrs Fiedling, got a blanket from his room and threw that over the ruined upholstery.

CHASE

When he sat down, the seat was lumpy beneath him, and he could not help but be reminded of the soft, lumpy look of Michael Karnes's corpse as it had lain on the grass in Kanackaway Park. Trying unsuccessfully to shake off that image, he drove off to keep his date.

Glenda Kleaver lived in a modestly expensive apartment on St John's Circle, on the third and highest floor. There was a peephole in her door, and she took the time to use it before answering his knock. She was wearing white shorts and a dark blue blouse, and she was in her bare feet, a casual note that served to make her shorter than him.

'You're very punctual,' she said. 'Come in.'

He stepped past her as she closed the door, and said, 'You live in a very nice neighbourhood here.'

She shrugged prettily. 'I'm one of those people who doesn't bother saving a dime. The way I figure it, I might die next week and not have gotten any fun out of a fat savings account – or, if I don't drop off, all my hard-earned nest egg will have been whittled away by the inflation. Those are my rationalizations, anyway.' She took his arm and led him to the couch, where she sat beside him. 'What could I get you to drink?'

'Scotch?'

'On the rocks?'

'Fine,' he said.

'Be right back.'

He watched her as she rose and crossed the room, disappeared down a short corridor that evidently led to the dining room and kitchen. In those shorts, her legs were phenomenal, so unbelievably long that he thought they looked as if they ought to twist and bend

127

like rubber. If Louise Allenby had remained in his thoughts at all, Glenda drove the girl out. There was clearly no chance of competition between them.

While she was gone, he looked over the large living room, which was decorated with ultra-modern furniture and fixtures. A crushed-velvet couch and two matching chairs, all the colour of cocoa. A stack of light-boxes against the far wall, not turned on at the moment. One light: a fifty-pound block of marble from which a twelve-foot steel pole curved out and ended in a silvery hood that could be twisted from one area of the room to another. A coffee table. A few bright paintings, a statue of a nude girl and boy embracing, a potted rubber plant that had grown almost to the ceiling. Nothing more. The tasteful combination of ultramodern and spare decoration was a feeling that he could agree with, and he felt comfortable here.

She came back with two glasses of Scotch and handed him one. This time, when she sat down, she took the chair directly across from the couch. That was actually better, he decided, than having her sit beside him, because he could appreciate those lovely legs more easily this way.

She said, 'Do you like fondue suppers?'

'I've never had one,' he said.

'Well, I'm sure you'll like it,' she said. 'If you don't like it, no more Scotch for you.'

Her laughed and settled back, at ease for the first time since he had come in.

Conversation was easy with her, and the subjects ranged from food to mixed drinks to furniture and design. She talked about the best places to go in town for dinner or for music, and he listened. He had been too much of a recluse to offer anything on the subject, but even if he had socialized a great deal, he would not have had much to add to what she had to say; she knew all the good places. He supposed she had a dozen suitors willing to pay her way anywhere she wished to go; she was exquisitely sensuous.

Dinner was delicious: baked potato, tossed salad, zucchini and the beef fondue that crackled and hissed as a background to their conversation. For dessert, there was crème de menthe pie, cherry liqueur to dawdle over.

'Shall we adjourn to the living room?' she asked.

He said, 'What about the dishes?'

'Let them sit,' she said.

'I'll help, and we'll get them done twice as fast.'

She stood up and put her napkin on the table. She said, 'You're the first man I've ever had to dinner who's offered to wash dishes.'

'I thought maybe I could *dry*,' he said.

She laughed. 'Still, you're unique.'

'Shall we get at them, then?'

'No,' she said. 'For one thing, I don't think guests should have to bother with that. For another, I'm not in the mood myself. I'd like to have a few more drinks and listen to music and watch the light-boxes while we talk.'

'Good enough,' Chase said. 'But later, the dishes.'

There were twelve light-boxes, each an eighteen-inch square, full of shifting patterns of red, blue, yellow, orange, white and green light. With no other lights burning, they cast strange images on the walls and ceilings and on the two of them as they sat together on the couch with their legs propped on the coffee table. Glenda's legs were covered with blue splashes, white squiggles, now a burst of red dots and concentric, wavery circles of yellow.

'You're not at all like I thought you'd be,' she said, terminating a lull in the conversation.

'How did you think I'd be?' he asked, not quite understanding what she meant.

'Oh, very gung-ho, very stern and conservative and cold, you know.'

'Is that the way I seemed when I came to your office?'

'No,' she said. 'I was surprised then. That's what I mean. Right from the start, you didn't act like a war hero, no swelled head, just very polite and a little bit shy.'

He could not manage to contain his surprise. 'You knew me from the very start?'

'Well, your picture *had* been on the front page twice that week.' She sipped her drink, put it down on the end table beside the sofa.

'But you never said anything.'

'I'm sure you're sick to death of being congratulated.'

'Yes,' he said. 'Even more sick than that.'

She said, 'When I came back from the storage room and saw you were gone, I thought you *were* angry about not being waited on when you should have been.'

'That wasn't it at all,' he said. 'I remembered another appointment that had slipped my mind, and I was already late.' Now, for the first time all evening, he remembered what he had come here for tonight: to question her about the people who had used the morgue Tuesday, about Judge. But he could not think of any reasonable way to broach the subject. Besides, he didn't want to. All he wanted was to go on like this, sitting side by side, drinking, talking, the music behind them and the lights ahead.

'Were you really looking for parts of your family history?'

'What else?' he asked.

'It just seemed out of character then,' she said. 'And twice as out of character now that I know you better.'

'Maybe I'm more complex than you suspect,' he said.

'I'm sure of it,' she said.

They watched the lights some more and said very little. There was actually no need to talk, for there was that easiness between them that allows no embarrassment at silence. She mixed them each another drink, and when she sat down again, she was closer to him than before.

Much later, after more conversation, more music, other silences and one more drink, she said, 'You are very much the gentleman, aren't you?'

'Me?'

'Yes.'

'I wouldn't have thought so.'

'The way you asked for a date on the telephone – and then offering to help with the dishes. Besides, if you weren't a gentleman, you would have made a pass at me by now.'

'Should I have?' he asked.

'Please do,' she said. She moved against him and tilted her head back, offering her lips to him and, perhaps later, everything.

He held her and kissed her for a long while. She was blue, spotted with yellow, edged with crimson as the light-boxes played.

'You kiss very well,' she said.

And perhaps he should have stopped at that point, before he had proven that there was nothing else at all he could do but kiss. He wanted her, and he thought that what he needed was bed with her, but he found that she was like a recorder of the past and that his touch activated the tapes; she radiated his memories of other women, dead women, became a history of his guilt. As herself, she was desirable, but as an archetype, she destroyed desire unknowingly.

'I'm sorry,' he said as they lay on her bed, staring at the dark ceiling that seemed, at times, only inches away from their faces.

'For what?' she asked. She was holding his hand, and he was glad for that.

'Don't humour me,' he said. 'You were expecting more.'

'Was I?' she asked, rising on one elbow and peering at him beside her in the gloom. 'Well, even if that's so, *you* were expecting more too. If I use your reasoning, *I* owe *you* an apology.'

His attitude toward her consideration was distinctly ambivalent, for though he appreciated the way she spared his feelings and tried to coax him into good humour, he *wanted* to be humiliated. He did not know exactly why he should feel that way.

He said, 'You're wrong about that, because I really wasn't expecting anything more.'

'Oh?'

'I haven't been able to,' he said. 'Not since – since I came back from Nam.' He had never told anyone but Dr Cauvel the history of his impotency, but now he seemed to be using it to elicit the scorn she had been withholding.

She moved closer to him, and rising further, began to gently brush the hair from his forehead. She said, 'That's a bitch all right, but it isn't everything. You can still stay the night, can't you?'

'After this?'

'I said this wasn't all,' she snapped. 'It would be very nice just to have someone to sleep with, to warm the other half of the bed. All right?'

'All right,' he said.

'Hungry?' she asked, changing the subject before he could find some other point to drag the original conversation on. 'Let's go fix an omelet.'

He gripped her hand more tightly than before and said, 'Wait a bit yet.' They lay side by side, quiet, as if listening. When he wasn't crying any more, he let her turn on the light, and they went to make a snack.

At breakfast the next morning, Chase said, 'If I – if we'd made love last night, would that have been normal for you?'

'Having a man overnight, on the first date?' she asked.

'Yes, that.'

'Not normal, no.'

'But it has happened before?'

She mopped up the yellow of her last egg with a piece of buttered toast. 'Twice before,' she said.

He finished his eggs and picked up his coffee. He said, 'I wish –'

'Stop it!' she said, with much more force in her quiet voice than he had heard before. 'You really are the masochist, aren't you?'

'Maybe.'

She leaned back, finished. 'But you'd like me to tell you it was something special with you, even though we didn't actually do anything.'

'No,' he said.

She smiled. 'That's a lie, Ben. You do want me to say it was something special, but you won't believe me if I say it was.'

'How could it have been?' he asked.

'It was,' she said. She blushed, a fact he found both old fashioned and delightful in such a liberated woman. 'Ben, it was rather special, and I like you very much.'

'Perhaps it wasn't special,' he said. 'Just different.'

'Bullshit.'

'The fact remains that we didn't –'

She interrupted him. 'I feel more comfortable with you, happier, more myself than I've ever felt with anyone in my life. And all of that, only the morning after our first date.'

'You feel comfortable because you feel safe.'

'A lie,' she said.

When he looked up a moment later, to see the cause of her abrupt answer and the ensuing silence, he was surprised to see tears in her eyes. He said, 'Okay, Glenda. I'm sorry. And I want to see you again, if that's all right with you.'

'Christ, you're dense,' she said. 'That's what I've been trying to get you to say all morning.'

At the door, he kissed her and found that it was not at all awkward, that they might have been long-time lovers.

She said, 'I'm sorry to have to drive you out so early,

but it's my mother's day to visit. I've got to straighten the place up and remove all traces of my illicit behaviour.'

'I'll call,' he said.

'If you don't, I'll call you.'

Outside, the day was bright and hot, and a breeze only barely stirred the trees by the kerb. In his present state of mind, however, no degree of uncomfortable weather could affect him. He got in the Mustang, rolled the window down to get some fresh air, and was slipping the key in the ignition when it happened. Behind him something snapped with a curiously brittle sound, followed by a solid *thump*. When he turned, he saw a bullet hole in the centre of the rear window. Judge was up early on this bright, warm day.

Chase fell sideways on the seat, below the level of the windows, with the back of the front seat to protect him from Judge's present position, and he heard the second shot star the back window in almost the same instant. On his side, with his head pressed against the vinyl of the passenger's seat, he could hear the slug slam into the upholstery, could feel the seat jerk a bit as it absorbed the shock. A silenced pistol was quiet, but it also packed less of a punch, since the extended, baffled muzzle cut the bullet's velocity appreciably. Ordinarily, it might have come through the thin stuffing of the bucket seat.

He waited long minutes for a third shot.

It did not come.

Cautiously, he raised his head and looked around. He could not see anything unusual, and he was not shot at again. He started the engine, pulled away from the kerb and tramped the gas hard.

CHASE

Twenty minutes later he was certain that he was not being followed, for he had driven so many side streets and made so many abrupt turns into alleyways while he watched the rearview mirror, that a tail could not help but reveal himself. He found the crosstown three-lane and headed home.

For a few hours he had forgotten Judge, though Judge had quite obviously not forgotten him. He was shaking badly, and he felt an itch at the back of his head about where the slug would have split his skull if Judge had been a better marksman. Indeed, he was shaking so badly that he twice thought he would have to stop the car and gather his wits. At first that seemed like an unreasonable response to the incident, especially for a man who had seen ground action in Southeast Asia. But then he realized that now he had something to lose, something to be afraid of being denied: hope, Glenda, whatever it was that might develop between them. He must not forget Judge again; he must be twice as careful as ever before.

It occurred to him, as he parked in front of the house, that Judge might have gone ahead, anticipating his destination to take a position here, waiting for Chase to return. He sat in the car a long while, unwilling to get out and test that theory. At last, when he realized that Judge could have shot him in the car as easily as on his way to the door, he got out.

In the downstairs hallway, Mrs Fiedling said, 'I hadn't realized you were going away overnight.'

'Neither had I,' Chase said.

She looked at his rumpled clothes as he kept walking toward the steps. 'You didn't have an accident, did you?'

'No,' he said, starting up the stairs. 'And I wasn't drinking, either.'

His attitude so surprised her that she didn't have anything to say until he was too far up the stairs to hear her.

In his room, he bolted the door and lay down on the bed. He let the shakes take him completely, until the fear was sweated out of him.

Nine

Two hours later Judge called. When Chase picked up the receiver, hoping it was Glenda, Judge said, 'Well, you were lucky again.'

Chase was not as calm as he had been the other times they'd talked, and he had to fight off the urge to slam the phone down. He said, 'You were just as bad a marksman as before, that's all.'

'I'll agree with that,' Judge said amicably enough. 'But it's also the fault of the bore on the silencer.'

Chase said, 'I have money. You know that. If I paid you off, would you let me alone?'

'How much?' Judge sounded eager.

'Five thousand,' Chase said.

'It's not enough.'

'Seven, then.'

'Ten,' Judge said. 'Ten thousand dollars, and I'll stop trying to kill you, Mr Chase.'

Chase felt himself smiling, a very tight smile but a

138

smile nonetheless. He said, 'Fine. How do I make the payment?'

Judge's voice was suddenly so loud and furious that Chase could only barely understand what he said. 'You bastard, don't you realize I can't be bought off, not with your money, not with anything in this world? You deserve to die, because you killed children and you're a fornicator, and you are going to be punished accordingly. I am not corrupt. I can't be bribed!'

Chase waited, listening as Judge regained control of himself. In the tone and fury of the tantrum, Judge's madness had been more evident than ever.

At last Judge said, 'Do you see my point?

'Yes.'

'Good!' Judge paused, sighed. 'I saw you going into her apartment, you know, and I can be certain that you spent the night in her bed, with that blonde slut.'

'She's no slut.'

'I know exactly who and what she is.'

'Oh?'

'Yes. She's that tall blonde slut from the *Press-Dispatch*. I saw her Tuesday when I was there looking over their back issues.'

'What does this have to do with our situation?' Chase asked.

'A great deal, because I've decided to kill her first.'

Chase was silent.

'Did you hear me, Chase?'

'You can't be serious.'

'Oh, but I am!'

Chase took a slow, deep breath, and said, 'You told me that you kill only those who deserve it, after researching their lives and learning all their sins. Are you breaking that rule now? Are you going to start killing indiscriminately?'

'She deserves to die,' Judge said. 'She's a fornicator. She let you stay the night with her, just the two of you, and she deserves to have judgment passed on her for that alone.'

'Is that why you called for the first time in three days, to tell me you'll kill her first?'

'Yes.'

'Why?'

'Do you like her, Chase?'

Chase said nothing.

'I hope you like her,' Judge said, 'because then it will be more fun to see how you react when I've finished with her.'

Chase waited, not daring to speak.

'Do you like her, Chase?'

'No.'

'That's a lie. I saw how you acted when you left her place, whistling and very jaunty – oh, very jaunty indeed!'

Chase said, 'I know who you are.

Judge laughed and said, 'I doubt that.'

'Listen. You're about my height, blond, with a long thin nose. You walk with your shoulders hunched forward, and you're a neat dresser. You are a perfectionist in the way you do things.'

'That's only a description,' Judge said. 'And not a particularly good one at that.'

'I think you're also a homosexual,' Chase said.

'That's not true!' Judge said, but he said it too vehemently. Evidently he realized that as well as Chase did, for he took a softer tone when he said,

'You've got wrong information.'

'I don't think so,' Chase said. 'I think I've just about got you nailed down.'

'No,' Judge said. 'You don't know my name, because if you knew it, you'd already have been to the cops.'

Chase said, 'Don't harm her.'

Judge only laughed again, deep and throaty, and hung up.

Chase tapped the buttons until he got the dial tone, looked up Glenda's number in the book and dialled it. She answered on the third ring. He said, 'I've got to see you.'

She hesitated a moment, then said, 'You sound serious. I hope you don't think we have to go through any more self-recrimination.'

'Not that,' he said. 'It's very important, Glenda, as important as life and death.'

She chuckled. 'That's one of the oldest lines in the book.'

'Please,' he said, 'I'm serious. I'm coming over.'

'You forget what day it is.'

'Your mother's still there?'

'Yes.'

'When will she leave?'

'After dinner.'

'That's too late!'

'Really, Ben,' she said, 'you're beginning to make me angry.'

He forced himself to wait a moment and to reply in a measured tone. 'Okay. But I'll be over at eight, if that's all right. Between now and then, don't answer your door for anyone you don't know, no matter how often he rings.'

She said, 'What's the matter?'

'I can't say now,' he told her. 'Will you do what I say?'

'Okay,' she said. 'See you at eight.'

Chase paced the room until he began to feel that he was only making the time drag by more slowly than ever. He went to the cupboard and took down his whisky bottle. It had lasted him several days already, but when he began to pour it, he knew that it would have to last several more, for he did not want to be the least bit fuzzy-headed tonight, not if the confrontation was to come soon. He corked the bottle, put it into the cupboard again, closed the cupboard door so that he could not see it, washed out the glass and dried it and put it away.

He realized, in this single decision, how much things had changed in such a short period of time.

He bathed, trying to take as long at it as he could, soaping and rinsing more than once.

He shaved, and then exercised.

When he looked at the clock, it read a few minutes after five.

Less than three hours until he could explain the situation to Glenda and offer whatever protection he could provide her. That was not so long, three hours. Except that she might be dead by then.

Ten

She was wearing a short green skirt and a dark blouse the colour of tobacco with a wing collar and puffed sleeves, eight buttons on each long cuff. Her yellow hair was drawn into a pair of ponytails, one just behind each ear, a device which made her, inexplicably, appear both childlike and sophisticated, though Chase supposed a visiting mother would notice only the innocence of the intended childish touch.

They kissed for a long while after she closed the door, as if their separation had been a few days rather than a matter of a few hours. Chase wondered, as he held her and felt her tongue in his mouth, how such a relationship between a man and a woman could develop in such a short time. It had not been love at first sight, of course, though not much less than that either. In short order, he had progressed from an immature and distant appreciation of her as a woman, through an unfulfilled desire for her as a sex object, through friendship and finally into love of a sort. Though they were not married, and though he could not physically possess her, he felt the confusion of emotion, love and lust and tenderness and a will to dominate her every moment, that supposedly plagued all newlywedded husbands. He imagined the two of them had found such a strong affinity for each other only because, psychologically, each of them gave something that the other required, but he did not want to delve into self-analysis very deeply. He simply wanted to enjoy, while holding most of the guilt at bay.

'Drink?' she asked when they broke apart.

'No,' he said. 'We have some serious talking to do first. Come here.'

On the couch, side by side, as they had started the previous evening, he said, 'Has anyone come to the door, anyone that you've never seen before?'

'No one,' she said.

'Any phone calls?'

'Just yours.'

'Good,' he said. But it was not a reprieve, only a postponement.

She took his hand in both of hers and said, 'Ben, what is it, what's the matter?'

'Nobody believes me,' he said. 'Because of Cauvel, the police won't listen to me.'

'I'll listen,' she said.

'You have to,' he said, 'because you're a part of it now.'

She waited a long time for him to continue, and when he did not say anything more, she said, 'Maybe I better get those drinks after all.'

'No,' he said, holding onto her. 'If I start drinking or

144

delay at all, I'll lose my nerve and not tell you.' He did not look at her again for twenty minutes, though he told her all of it, even about Operation Jules Verne and the tunnel. And the bamboo grate. And the women, all of it, right through to Judge's latest threat.

'Now I *need* a drink,' she said.

He didn't stop her. When she came back with two, he took his and said, 'Does this change anything? I guess it has to.'

'Change what?' she asked.

'Us.'

'Why should it change us?' she asked, and she seemed genuinely perplexed by the statement.

'But now you know what I am, what I've done, my part in the killing of those women.'

'That wasn't you,' she said.

'I shot like the rest.'

'Listen to me,' she said, and she spoke more earnestly, more firmly than he had ever heard her, the softness of her voice like a tiny but forcefully driven hammer, rapping out words so there would be no mistake about them. 'When you were over there in Vietnam, there were two Benjamin Chases. There was the Ben who took his orders seriously and carried them out because he had been raised to believe that every authority was right and that disobedience was some indication of spinelessness or subversiveness, the Ben who was further affected by fear that reinforced this respect for authority because the fear told him he would die on his own. Then there was the other Ben, the one who knew right and wrong, good and evil, instinctively, beyond the interference that his society had built into his moral judgments. That's the Ben I know, the second one. He has spent well over a year trying to destroy the remnants of the other Ben, the one who obeyed this Zacharia, and he's gone through hell to cleanse himself. The first Ben *is* dead. The war killed him, one of the few good kills that damn stupid war has made. And now there is no reason on earth why the second Ben, my Ben, should be ashamed of himself or want to be punished. And there's even less of a reason why I should hold anything that the dead Ben did against my own Ben.' She paused and blushed, evidently surprised at her own verbosity, and looked at her round knees. 'That's simplified, but it's me. Can you understand what I'm saying?'

'Yes,' he said. He took her in his arms and kissed her then, for he could not see anything else to do.

When his hands slipped down over her breasts and began to massage her full hips, he realized abruptly that he was only leading them toward another point of frustration. He pulled back, and directing the conversation to Judge again, said, 'Have you thought of anything I might have overlooked, even the smallest lead?'

'Not really,' she said. 'I recognized him from your description, but I don't know his name or anything else about him.' She took a swallow of her drink and suddenly put it down. 'Did you ask Louise Allenby if anyone had been bothering her and the dead boy – maybe weeks and weeks prior to the murder? If Judge really followed them around doing his "research," they might have noticed him or had a run-in with him.'

Chase said, 'I'd suspect they never even noticed him. Besides, the police would probably have thought to ask.'

'They don't know nearly as much as you do, nothing at all about this "research" angle.'

'True enough,' he said. 'I'll give her a call. If she's home, we can go right out there.'

She was home, and she was pleased to hear from him. At ten o'clock Chase and Glenda left the apartment and went down to the Mustang.

The night was quiet and far less muggy than the day had been. Chase was conscious, in the pools of darkness, of all the places where a man with a gun might hide.

He had argued that there was no need for her to accompany him, that it was folly for the two of them to walk out the front of the building together, but he could not make her see it his way. She had said, 'If we're too frightened to go outside, Judge has already won, in a way, hasn't he?' Chase had tried to explain what a .32-calibre bullet would do to her if placed properly, but she had countered with the observation that he had made earlier – Judge was a poor shot.

When he stepped off the kerb with her to walk her to the door, she said, 'No need to play the courtly gentleman. I hate men opening doors for me as if I'm an invalid.'

'What if the gentleman enjoys being courtly?' he asked.

'Then he can take me somewhere that I have to wear a long ball gown, where I *need* help.'

He let go of her arm. 'Very well, Miss Liberation. But can we get inside, out of sight?'

'You think he may be watching from a nearby roof? He'd have to have an awfully good eye to shoot in this darkness.'

'Just the same,' he said, turning away from her and going to the driver's door, which he opened a split second before she began to open hers. In that split second, he knew that something was terribly wrong. . .

He had left the car locked. She should not have been able to open her door until he had reached across and pushed up the latch stem.

'Don't move!' he shouted across the roof of the Mustang.

She responded much better than he could have hoped. She did not continue instinctively to open the door, as most would have, thinking the danger behind her. If she had opened the door any wider, she would have been dead a moment later.

'What is it?' she asked.

'He's been in the car.'

'Judge?'

'Yes.' He cleared his throat. His mouth was dry, and his tongue stuck to the roof of it when he tried to speak. 'Don't open your door any wider. Let it go slowly back into place, but don't slam it or shut it tightly.'

'Why?'

'I believe he's wired explosives to your door.'

She was silent for a long moment, and when she finally spoke, she was genuinely frightened for the first time. 'How can you tell?'

'When I opened my door, the overhead light came on. From here, I can see a single strand of heavy-duty wire leading from the window knob on your door into the glove compartment. The explosives must be in there, for he's taken out the bulb in the glove-compartment door and left the door open.'

'But how in the world did you–?'

'We used to check a car in Nam before we got in. The Cong used the routine on us regularly.'

She had been slowly releasing the door as they conversed, and now she let go of it as it came to rest against the frame.

'Now walk away from the car and get back by the building.'

'What are you going to do?'

'Disarm it,' Chase said.

'I won't let you–'

'I've done it a dozen times before,' he said. 'Now do as I told you.'

When she was far enough back to be safe from any accidental explosion, Chase opened his door the rest of the way and sat down in the driver's seat.

A white panel delivery truck roared by, leaving a wake of sealike echoes that shushed back and forth between the brick walls of the apartment houses.

Chase leaned over the console between the bucket seats and peered into the open glove compartment. Even in the weak light, he could see the pebbled curve of the grenade. It had been taped securely to the shelf the glove-compartment door made when it lay open, then further bound by lengths of heavy-gauge wire that encompassed the width and breadth of the small door. The wire knotted around the window knob on the passenger's door led directly to the steel arming ring at the top of the grenade and was twisted around that bright loop many times.

Chase got out of the car and went to the apartment house steps where Glenda was waiting. 'Do you have any household tools? A pair of pliers would be the thing.'

'Needlenose pliers?' she asked. 'I have a pair of those that came with my Christmas tree lights.'

'Good enough,' he said.

While she was gone, he stood by the steps with his hands in his pockets, trying not to think what the grenade would have done to her. He might have been hurt himself, but she would have been literally torn apart as the sheet metal of the Mustang door shattered like glass.

She came back with the pliers. 'How long?' she asked.

'Five minutes,' he said. 'Wait right here. I don't think we have to worry about Judge for the moment. He'll have been confident the explosion would finish us off.'

In the car again, he leaned over the console and caught the trigger wire in the back jaws of the pliers, squeezed the handles shut and began to twist back and forth as rapidly as he could manage. There was actually little danger of exploding the hand grenade now, though he would not feel safe until the trigger wire had been severed. Judge had given the lead at least ten inches of slack, a generous safety margin for all the work that Chase had to do.

Judge had not intended to make the disarming process easier by providing the slack, of course. His purpose had been to insure that Glenda had partly opened the door before the grenade could go off, so that the full force of the explosion would strike her more directly. Indeed, with that much slack, and the seven seconds between the pin-pull and the detonation, she might even have slid inside and sat down without noticing the wire, aware of the danger

150

only when it was too late to escape.

The trigger wire snapped in two as Chase applied one last, hard twist to it.

He put the pliers down and crawled over the console, sat in the passenger's seat. He opened that door to let some of the streetlight flood in, and then set to work snipping the wires that bound the grenade in place. Those and the strips of black electrician's tape came away with litle problem. When he freed the metal pineapple and tested its weight, there was no longer any doubt in his mind that it was a live piece and not just a stage prop Judge had put there for a laugh.

Chase wrapped the grenade in the chamois waxing cloth that had come with the car and tucked it into the glove compartment, which he locked.

He got out of the car, unwound the wire from the window knob and pushed that under the seat, closed the door and walked to the steps. 'It's all done.'

'Where's the dynamite?' she asked.

'No dynamite, just a hand grenade. I wrapped it and locked it in the glove compartment.'

She looked ill, the colour gone from her face. 'Is that safe?'

'Perfectly safe. It can't go off unless someone yanks the pin loose.'

'Where could he have gotten a hand grenade?'

'I don't know,' Chase said. 'I guess there are a number of ways. I intend to find out some day.'

'What do we do now?' she asked.

'We go see Louise Allenby, like we planned. Now it seems even more urgent to track down that bastard.'

In the car, as he started the engine, she said, 'I must

congratulate you on your good nerves. This hardly seems to have upset you at all.'

'It did, though,' he said. 'I don't think I've ever been so upset in my life.' He knew he had to conserve himself for hate, hate directed toward Judge, hate that would benefit him if he nurtured it.

Louise Allenby answered the door wearing the tops of blue-flowered pyjamas that barely covered her below the curve of her ass, and she had a very slick come-hither look for him. She said, 'I knew you'd be back to get the reward —' Then she saw Glenda and said, 'Oh!'

'May we come in?' Chase said.

She stepped back, confused, closed the door after them.

Chase introduced Glenda as a close friend, though he felt that Louise saw instantly past the description. Her face soured into a pout that was not at all the woman but completely the child she was.

She said, 'Will you have a drink this time?'

'No,' Chase said. 'We've only got a couple of questions, and we'll be going.'

'*I'm* drinking tonight,' she said. She flounced across the room and made herself something Chase could not identify. She stood with her right hip cocked so that the pyjama tops pulled up slightly on her round, firm buttocks, soft and white against the tan of her legs. When she came back, she sat down in such a fashion that for a brief moment it was all there and visible and pretty, then swung one leg over the other and shut down the best part of the show. 'What are your questions?'

Chase felt uncomfortable, but he could tell that Glenda was enjoying his embarrassment and the girl's anger. She sat on one of the stiff chairs, looking exceedingly delicious, her own legs crossed and much more fetching than Louise's legs for all the younger girl's nakedness.

Chase said, 'You said you'd gone with Mike for a year before – before he was murdered.'

'That's about right,' she said. She looked at Glenda, looked down at her legs, frowned just the slightest, then returned her gaze to Chase and never took it from him until he got up to leave. 'What about it?'

'In that time, did you ever notice anyone following you – as if they were keeping a watch on you?'

'Recently? No.'

'Not just recently,' he said. 'Even weeks ago, or months ago.'

She hesitated, sipped her drink and said, 'The beginning of the year, about February and March, there was something like that.'

Chase felt his throat catch, and he did not want to speak for fear that it would all prove to be nothing and would put them right back where they had been when they walked in the door. At last he said, 'What do you mean?'

'Well, when Mike first said he was following us, I just laughed, you know?' She frowned, remembering how she had laughed and wondering now if she had not been all wrong. 'The idea was silly, right out of a movie. Mike was like that, too, always off on one fantasy or another. He was going to be a painter, did you know? At first he was going to work in a garret and become famous. Then he was going to be a paperback-book illustrator and then a very famous industrial designer. He never could decide – but he knew whatever it was he would be famous and rich. A dreamer.' She shook her head, so wise with hindsight, knowing that dreams and plans don't work.

'What about being followed?' Chase asked. He did not want to anger her by prodding her the wrong way, for he knew she had the kind of temper that might make her clam right up. On the other hand, he didn't want to spend the rest of the night listening to a biography of Michael Karnes.

'It was a man in a Volkswagen,' she said. 'A red Volkswagen. After a week or so of listening to Mike, I started watching myself, and I found out it wasn't another fantasy. There really was someone following us in a red Volkswagen.'

'What did he look like?' Chase asked.

'I never saw him. He stayed far enough behind and always parked far along the kerb when we went in somewhere. But Mike knew him.'

Chase felt, for an instant, as if the top of his head were coming off, and he wanted to reach out and shake the rest of it out of her without having to go through this question-and-answer routine. Calmly he said, 'Who was the man in the VW?'

'I don't know,' she said. 'Mike wouldn't tell me.'

'And you weren't curious?' he asked.

'Sure I was. But when Mike made up his mind about something, he wouldn't change it. One night, when we went to the Diamond Dell – that's a drive-in hamburger joint on Galasio – he got out of the car and went back and talked to the man in the VW. When he came back, he said he knew him and that we wouldn't have any more trouble with him. And he was right. The man drove away, and he didn't follow us any more. I never knew what it was about.'

'But you must have had some idea,' Chase insisted. 'You can't have let it drop without finding out something more concrete.'

She put her drink down. She said, 'Mike didn't want to talk about it, and I thought I knew why. He never said directly, but I think the man in the VW had made a pass at him.'

'A homosexual,' Chase said.

'I only think so,' she said. 'I couldn't prove it.' She started to pick up her drink, then brightened. 'Hey, do you think it was the same man Monday night, the one with the ring?'

'Maybe,' Chase said.

'Who is he?'

'I don't know yet. But I'm going to find out.' He stood up, and Glenda stood up beside him.

Louise said, 'I'll just bet that's who it was!'

'One more thing,' Chase said. 'I'd like a list of Mike's friends, anyone his own age that he was close to.'

'Girl friends too?' she asked, just the slightest bit tart about it.

He thought a moment and decided that this was not something a boy Mike's age would discuss with girls he was dating, for fear the very idea of having been approached by a homosexual would call his own masculinity into question. With boys his own age, however, he might be inclined to bring it up as a joke, for laughs. 'Just boys,' he said.

'How many?'

'Five or six.'

'That would probably be a waste. Mike wasn't close to very many people. I can only think of three guys, actually.'

'That'll do.'

She got a piece of paper at the desk, sat down and printed the three names. She got up, put the pen away and brought the list back to him. All the getting up and sitting down was designed, he was sure, to give him a few more little glimpses of what she must have considered paradise.

'Thanks,' he said, seeing addresses below the names and wondering how many of Mike's best friends had been to bed with her.

At the door, Louise brushed against him, all plastic promise and manufactured musk. She whispered, 'You know, it could have been very nice indeed.'

Glenda was in front of Chase with her back to them, and she should not have been able to hear, but she turned and smiled pleasantly at the younger girl. She said, not pleasantly, 'But the problem is that you try too hard, Louise, really you do.'

Louise coloured, twisted away from them in unconscious – for the first time that evening – display of flesh and slammed the door in their faces.

'She's just a girl, after all,' Chase said, looking sideways at her. But Glenda showed no sign of understanding his point. 'Did you have to be like that with her?'

'She doesn't *act* like a young girl,' Glenda snapped. 'Not one bit like.'

He realized that she was jealous, and if circumstances had not been so tense, he might have taken the time to enjoy that.

In the car again, she seemed to have calmed down. She said, 'What's next, Detective Chase?'

Chase sat behind the wheel, staring at the dark street and thinking about Judge. He had taken pains to be certain no one had followed them from Glenda's apartment, but he could not escape the feeling that there was a gun trained on the back of his head – or on the back of hers. The ordeal with the grenade had put him on a keen edge.

He said, 'Let's see if any of these boys are home.'

'At eleven of a Sunday evening?'

'I guess not,' Chase said. 'But it can't hurt to try.' He drove away, glancing repeatedly in the rear-view mirror. There was no one following them, at least not in the physical sense.

Jerry Taylor, the third boy on the list, was at home. He lived with his parents in the Braddock Heights part of the city, in a two-storey stone house set on a luxuriously planted full-acre lot. Braddock Heights provided 'gracious' living for professional people and their families, doctors and lawyers and the more successful businessmen. The man who answered the door, tall and greying, dressed in casual slacks, a white shirt and a tattered sweater, did not seem surprised that his son should be visited by two adults at that hour of the night. He asked if Jerry was in trouble, nodded when they said it was nothing like that, escorted them downstairs to the game room and said Jerry would be along in a few minutes. He left, and he did not return with his son.

Jerry Taylor was a thin, intense boy with hair that fell to his somewhat stooped shoulders. He was wearing bell-bottom jeans and a workshirt, and he assumed a posture of disinterest from the moment he walked in the door, though that was clearly against his very nature. He listened to Chase, answered his questions, provided nothing new and escorted them upstairs and into the night again. They might just as well have been ghosts passing through unnoticed. As they walked to the car, the stone house stood behind them like a fortress.

'I wonder if all his friends are that outgoing,' Glenda said.

'Generational preoccupation.'

'Boredom?' she asked.

'No,' Chase said. '*Appearing* bored. They want to look as if they've seen and heard it all.'

'You talk like you're forty years his senior.'

'I feel like it, too.'

She patted his shoulder. 'What next?'

'How old are you?' he asked.

'My, good God, what tact the man has!'

'I'm sorry,' he said, putting his arm around her. 'But I'm not being nosey, and I do have a reason.'

'Twenty-one,' she said.

'Older than I thought,' he said.

'So throw me out of the car.'

He laughed. 'I just wondered what the most popular local hang-outs for eighteen- and nineteen-year-olds were. I'm sure they changed in the years I've been away. And they probably aren't the same as they were when you were that age. A year or two is a long time for an "in" spot to stay "in".'

'The hamburger places out on Galasio are always popular. But I'd say the chances of your finding one of the two boys are phenomenally small.'

'Agreed,' he said. 'We might as well go back to your place and wait. If I can't catch either of them tonight, by phone, we'll check them out in the morning.'

'Tomorrow's Monday,' Glenda said. 'Work for me.'

He said, 'Do you have any sick leave coming?'

'Seven days–'

'Take one.'

'But–'

'Otherwise, I'll have to come to work and sit with you to know you're safe, and I won't get anything done on this.'

She thought a moment, said, 'Okay. Now let's go home; I feel all creepy sitting out here in the open.'

At her apartment, he made sure the door was locked and that the chain latch was also properly in place. He drew the drapes on all the windows and tested the sliding glass terrace doors, though it didn't seem likely that Judge would lasso one of the terrace railings and climb three floors on a rope. It was as simple as that in melodramas, but rarely in real life.

'Scotch,' she said, handing him a glass.

They turned out all the lights, turned on the light-boxes against the far wall and sat on the floor with their backs against the sofa, watching the changing patterns.

She said, 'Maybe now you have enough to go to the police.'

'The grenade?'

'Yes.'

'You forget that I was in the army. If they live up to their past performance, they'll say I brought it back to the States, illegally, and they'll slam me in jail for a few days.'

'Without the grenade, then?' she said. 'Maybe you still have enough to give them.'

'What? The fact that he wore a pinkie ring, that Mike's girl friend says she thinks he made a pass at Mike, that someone got a university report on me by using a false name?' He tasted the Scotch. 'We still haven't got a name.'

'A description, though?'

'They'll say it's something else, or that I'm making it up.' He put his drink down on the coffee table at his side. 'I won't give them the chance to treat me like that again. When I go back to them, it'll be to make them eat their own – own hats.'

Glenda laughed and drew up her knees. 'Hats, huh?'

He smiled and said, 'Look, we can't do anything more until we talk to those boys, and they're probably not home yet. Let's just take a little while to relax and talk about other things. For instance, I don't really know what books you read, what kind of music you like, whether or not you like to go dancing–'

'Oh, brother,' she said, 'are you asking to be bored.'

But he was not bored as the evening went on, for he found a freshness in her outlook that lifted his own spirit and made his problems fade. Now and again they kissed, and he sat with his arm around her, but they did not begin necking. It was almost as if they had made a tacit agreement to forgo even that degree of serious contact at least until this affair had come to a conclusion and Judge had been located.

Forty-five minutes later the telephone rang.

Chase said, 'Damn those persistent ex-suitors of yours!'

'More likely my mother,' she said.

She went to the phone and picked it up. 'Hello . . . Yes?' She was silent a moment, listening. 'I don't like this.' More silence. 'Now it's your turn to listen to me–' She stopped in mid-sentence, stared at the receiver for a moment and hung up.

'Wasn't your mother, was it?' Chase asked teasingly.

'No,' she said. 'It was Judge. He wanted to tell me that he knows what we're probably doing in here. He said he'd kill me first, then you, then Louise Allenby. He congratulated you on finding and disarming the grenade, and he says it won't be so simple the next time. He told me to have a pleasant evening.'

Eleven

Norman Bates, Mike Karnes's friend whose name was first on Louise Allenby's list, was at home when Chase called him shortly after midnight, though he twice said he had been on his way to bed when the phone rang and was not even as cooperative as Jerry Taylor. In the end, it did not matter if he wanted to cooperate or not, because he had never heard Mike mention any homosexual advances or any man who had followed him around.

The last boy, Martin Cable, was in bed. His mother said, 'He works six days a week during the summer, and he needs his sleep.'

'I'd only take five minutes of his time,' Chase said.

'He's already asleep. I won't wake him now.'

He said, 'Could you tell me where he works?'

She said, 'You the same man who called here earlier?'

'Yes,' he said.

162

CHASE

She was silent a moment, then said, 'He starts at eight in the morning at Governor's Place Apartments. He's one of the lifeguards at the pool.'

'Thank you,' he said, but he realized that she had already hung up.

'No luck?' Glenda asked.

'We'll have to see him in the morning.'

She yawned. 'To bed, then. What with my mother's visit and the little scene with the grenade, I can hardly keep my eyes open.'

In bed, they held each other for a while, but they both knew the night was only for sleeping. It was the first night in many months that Chase did not dream at all.

At eight-thirty there were two young men at the apartment complex pool, one of them polishing the metalwork above the waterline while the other scrubbed the white diving board preparatory to opening for business at ten o'clock. They watched Glenda with unconcealed interest, and Chase wondered if they shouldn't be taught some manners. When one of them whistled, however, Chase saw that Glenda only smiled, accepting as flattery what his mother would have called rudeness. It was another of the little differences of perspective between them that made Chase feel old and tired.

Chase went to the boy polishing the ladder at the shallow end of the pool. 'Martin Cable?'

'That's Marty,' the boy said, pointing to the guard on the driving board.

Martin Cable was lean but muscular, his arms bulging modestly even when they weren't flexed, tighter and stringier than a weight lifter. He had a lot of dark hair that covered his ears and the nape of his neck, but his face still held no sign of a beard. He sat up on the board as they approached, slightly above them.

'Martin Cable?' Chase asked.

'Yes?' He had none of Jerry Taylor's attitude of boredom and appeared willing to be friendly, unlike Norman Bates. The sun, reflected by the water, made odd, shimmering spots on his face and chest.

'I understand you were a friend of Mike Karnes.'

'Of a sort.'

'I've got some questions I'd like to ask, if you can spare a few minutes.'

The boy glanced at Glenda, let his gaze travel down to her slim ankles and then work its way leisurely back up again. While he enjoyed the view, he made up his mind and said, 'Yeah, sure, ask away.'

'How well did you know Mike?'

'Close friends, shared his car sometimes for double dates.'

'Same year in school?'

'Yeah. Graduated together June a year ago.'

'Was Mike a terror with the girls?' Chase asked.

'Was he ever!' the boy said. 'Christ!'

'I had heard that besides Louise Allenby, he kept several other girls on the string.'

'Not only on the string,' Cable said. 'But satisfied. He just couldn't get enough of it, maybe because it was still so new to him.'

'New?' Chase asked. He thought they were both talking about the same thing, but now he wasn't sure.

'He got his first piece when he was a junior, the last day of school that year. Overnight he changed from a bashful, sportsminded teenage boy into – well, a stud. You know how that is, you ever see it happen to someone?'

'Yes,' Chase said.

'We told him he'd wear it out if he didn't slow down.'

It seemed the proper moment to broach the main topic without forcing him to clam up, since they had already established Mike Karnes's claim to manhood. 'Did he ever tell you about another man – making a pass at him?'

'A queer?'

'Yes.'

He looked at Glenda again, back at Chase, mulling over the possibilities. He said, 'You haven't told me who you are.'

Chase told him, introduced Glenda.

'That doesn't explain this sudden interest in Mike.'

Chase said, 'I don't think the police are doing anything on the case. You know my connection with it. I don't relish having a madman running around loose with a grudge against me.'

Cable nodded. When he spoke, a moment later, his words were quick and run together, as if he were betraying a trust and wanted to get it over with as quickly as he could. 'Two years ago Mike got laid for the first time, and everything slipped a little for him after that. If you know his parents, you understand how it could happen. They'd never let on to him that there was anything fun in life, let alone something like sex. He just sort of broke loose, all at once. After that, his grades dropped.'

'When was this?'

'Just past the middle of the second semester of our

senior year. He wanted to get into State, but he wasn't going to make it if he showed as poorly in the second term as in the first. Physics was his worst subject, and when it got really bad, he started taking sessions with a tutor.'

'And who was that?' Chase asked.

'A teacher who did that kind of thing Saturdays. I never knew his name, never saw him.'

'And this was the man who made a pass at Mike?'

'Yeah. I only heard about it a year later. Mike pulled his marks up and scraped into State as a day student, and I went away to Pitt. Neither of us wrote much, but we always got together when I came home over weekends or on holidays. In February we doubledated with these red-headed twins Mike knew from State, very nice stuff. On our way back to the city, after we'd let them off for the night, he told me about this character who was following him everywhere he went.'

'His physics tutor?'

'That's right.'

'What did Mike tell you about him; even the smallest detail might be more important than it seems.'

Cable squinted his eyes, licked his lips. He said, 'He quit the Saturday morning tutoring sessions because this guy kept trying to convince him there would be nothing wrong in their going to bed together. That had been nearly a year earlier, when we were both seniors. Since then, Mike said, this guy kept bothering him, periodically, trying to talk to him. He always hung up when the guy called. So then he started following Mike everywhere he went, a real creep.'

'But you don't remember his name?'

'No.'

'Not even first name.'

'Not even that much.'

'Nickname?'

'Mike certainly wasn't on nickname terms with him!'

'I suppose not.'

'That's it,' Cable said. He laced his hands together and cracked his knuckles. 'I wish there was more.'

'I think that's enough, just what I needed,' Chase said.

'Good.' Cable turned from Chase, tossed his head to flip his thick hair out of his face, smiled at Glenda. He said, 'You've got fantastic legs.'

'Thank you,' she said.

The sun made her seem like a mirage, heat waves rippling up from the pavement as she walked toward the car. She was beautiful, Chase thought, and Cable had been right about her legs. He wondered, suddenly, whether he would ever help her fulfil the promise of her body, be a man to her in bed. He quickly avoided further thoughts of that nature as she got into the car.

'You're lovely,' he said.

'My God, a compliment!' she said in mock surprise. 'I thought I wouldn't hear one of those more than every other day or so.'

'I don't verbalize well,' he said. 'But that boy made me jealous. I saw how your face lighted when he said he liked your legs.'

'I may be a liberated woman, but I still have an ego.'

'I'll try to do better by it,' he said, touching her bare knee. The flesh was cool and firm. It generated such a powerful mixture of desire and guilt that he quickly let go of her. 'Did you get it?'

CHASE

She opened an envelope and took out six mimeographed sheets. 'A list of all the teachers in the system, high school and junior high schools and grade schools.'

'Address and phone number for each name,' he said. 'How did you do it?'

'A trick I learned from being around reporters too much.' She leaned forward and punched the lighter in the dash, took a cigarette from her purse, started it smoking. She took one deep drag and then was content to hold it. 'I met the Superintendent of Schools and passed myself off as the representative of a commercial mailing-list firm. He was so frustrated about having to work the summer while the teachers had off and so surprised to have a chance to talk to a nice young woman in a miniskirt, that he didn't question why we were doing business first-hand rather than by mail. I wrote a check on my personal account to pay for the list, and I didn't even have to explain that. Twenty-five dollars for name and address and telephone number of nearly three hundred employees – and they've probably sold the list half a dozen times so far this year, always for better money than that.'

He shook his head admiringly. 'With that sort of mind, you don't really need those legs.'

'Wrong.'

'Wrong?'

'Without the legs to look at, he would have been thinking more clearly. There would have been a number of very embarrassing questions.'

Chase gave the list back to her. 'Thanks to your legs, we're getting closer to home base.'

'You really think he's a physics teacher?'

'It fits in a lot of ways. Including the fact that it explains how he might possess a silencer for a pistol. He could have machined it himself, with a bit of patience and the application of his own special knowledge. I remember him blaming his bad aim on the bore of the silencer.'

Chase drove back to her apartment. Together they went over the list, circling the names of the physics instructors – three in all. He dialled all of them inside of ten minutes and managed to speak a few words with each. None of them sounded like Judge.

On the off chance that a physics tutor might not necessarily teach the subject in his regular job, they circled the names of senior and junior high school science teachers and phoned all thirty-nine of them. Twelve did not answer their phones, and four others were not at home but were expected back before dinner. None of the other twenty-three sounded like Judge.

By six-thirty they were satisfied with all but one man: Charles Shienbluth, a junior high school general science instructor. When Chase dialed his number for the seventh time, however, the man answered. 'Shienbluth speaking.'

'Is this the Mr Shienbluth who teaches science at Walterson Junior High School?' Chase asked.

'Yes, that's me.'

'Charles Shienbluth?'

'Yes. Who is this?'

Chase hung up.

'Well?' she asked.

He said, 'It wasn't Judge. It's all been another false lead.'

Twelve

Anne and Harry Karnes lived in a modest white frame house on Winkler Street, one of the older middle-class residential developments on the north side of the city. There was a three-year-old Rambler parked in the gravelled drive, and lights shone in the front room downstairs. Gauzy yellow curtains kept Chase from seeing anything of the room beyond the windows, but he supposed it would be as plain as the house and the block the house was set in. The only sounds were those made by trucks on the super-highway three blocks west and by a television set turned too loud in one of the nearby houses.

Glenda said, 'Are we going in or not?'

'I've been thinking,' Chase said, 'that maybe the homosexual angle doesn't have anything to do with this.'

'But the man following them drove a red Volkswagen, according to Louise Allenby. And you said he overreacted when you confronted him with the accusation on the telephone.'

'But gay people are supposedly less violent than straights. And the ones I've known bear that out. I can't picture any of the gay men I've met picking up a knife and killing.'

'The lover scorned,' she said.

'That's too trite to be acceptable.'

She slid closer to him, ignoring the console between the bucket seats. 'What's the matter, Ben? You're just making excuses to keep from going in and talking to Mike's parents.'

He looked at the lighted windows and sighed. 'They're going to want to thank me for trying to save their son's life, and it's going to be the hero thing all over again. I'm tired of that.'

'Maybe it'll be different,' she said. 'Anyway, if you want, I can go in alone.'

'It'd seem odd,' he said. 'They don't know you, who you are.' He opened the car door and put a foot on the kerb. 'Come on, let's get this over with.'

Anne Karnes answered the door, a grey-haired woman who wore no make-up and would not have benefitted by it very much even if she had. Her face was harsh, all angles and flat planes, her eyes set too close together by a fraction, her mouth too prim and thin-lipped. She was wearing a shapeless housedress that fell to the middle of her stocky calves, not out of any consciousness of fad styles, but because it was the kind of thing she had, apparently, always worn.

'Please come in,' she said. 'I've very glad to meet you.'

Grey. The inside of the house was grey, sad, quiet.

CHASE

The living-room furniture was heavy and dark, the arms of the chairs and sofas overlaid with white antimacassars. Two lamps burned, both shedding pale light, colourless light. The television was on, but one had the feeling that it was *always* on and that no one really watched it. The walls were the same tan colour of the walls in public institutions like schools and city hall corridors. Half a dozen motto plaques dressed the walls to conform with the styling of their tenants.

Harry Karnes was as grey as his wife and the room, a short man, slight of build. His hands shook when they were not resting on the arms of his easy chair, and he could not look directly at Chase, but stared slightly over his left shoulder.

Chase and Glenda sat on the sofa, leaning away from the back, distinctly uncomfortable in a room of slipcovers, antimacassars and prominently displayed Bibles. Mrs Karnes kept casting disapproving glances at the expanse of bare legs showing from beneath Glenda's miniskirt, while Mr Karnes studiously pretended that he didn't even know Glenda was a woman. The whole mood was vaguely similar to that in a funeral parlour.

When they were finally done with the thank-yous and Chase could change the course of the conversation, he said, 'The reason I came by was to ask you a few questions about Mike. You see, I don't believe the police are looking into this very thoroughly, and I'm anxious to see it settled – seeing as how the killer might well have a grudge against me.'

'What sort of questions?' Mrs Karnes asked.

Somewhere in an upstairs hallway a grandfather clock chimed, the brass notes hollow and faint, like

172

scraps of an agonizing nightmare.

'Mostly about his schoolwork,' Chase said.

'He was a good boy,' Mr Karnes said. 'He was good in school, and he was going to college too.'

'Let's not lie to Mr Chase,' Anne said, speaking twice as forcefully as her husband. 'We know that isn't right.'

'But he was a good boy,' the old man said, but sounded as if he were trying to convince himself as much as her.

'He went wild,' Mrs Karnes said. 'He went wild, and you'd not have thought he was the same boy from one year to the next.'

'How did he go wild?' Chase asked.

'Running around,' Mrs Karnes said. 'Out later than he should be, and usually with a girl. You know where he was killed, in that sinful place they call a park.'

Not wanting to pursue that line, Chase said, 'I came mainly to ask you about a tutor Mike had in physics during his senior year in high school.'

'He was out every night, and his grades went bad,' Mrs Karnes said. 'We tried everything we knew. What he needed was a good whipping, but he was bigger than either me or his father. When a boy grows up and loses respect for his elders, what can you do? He'd worked, and he had money for the car. Once he had that, there was no holding him down.'

Mr Karnes said nothing, but turned and stared at the television set, where a dog act was progressing in tediously predictable fashion.

'Who was his physics tutor?' Chase asked.

Mrs Karnes looked at the television as a dog leaped through a hoop and as another poodle did a back flip.

As the unseen audience applauded, she said, 'I can't remember his name. Do you, Dad?'

Her husband looked away from the set and stared over Chase's shoulder. 'I never met him,' he said.

'Did you pay by cheque? You'd have had to make out the cheques to someone.'

'Paid in cash,' Mrs Karnes said. 'It was eight dollars for a two-hour session every Saturday morning, and Mike took the money with him. After a while the tutor got interested in Mike's physics ability and offered to teach him free.'

'Mike was a smart boy,' the old man said. 'He could have been something someday.'

'If he hadn't gone wild,' his wife half agreed. 'But he did go wild, and he wouldn't have settled down enough to accomplish beans.'

Chase felt Glenda's foot brush against his, and he knew that she was as bothered as he was by the low-key, continuing argument between the husband and wife – and by their unsympathetic approach to their only child's weaknesses, if weaknesses they were.

He said, 'How did you go about locating a private instructor – or was he someone from Mike's high school?'

'We got his name from the high school,' she said. 'They have a list of recommended tutors. But he didn't teach there. I think he taught in a Catholic school.'

'It was a private school,' Harry Karnes said, rallying a bit, 'not a Catholic school. One of the academies in the city.'

'A boys' school?' Chase asked.

'I believe so.'

'I'm still sure it was a parochial school,' his wife said.

She stared at the old man as if to force him to retract his statement.

'You don't, by chance, remember the name of the school, do you?' Chase asked the old man, the tired old man.

'No,' Harry Karnes said. 'But it wasn't parochial. I remember, at the time, how Anne was afraid he might be Catholic. She didn't want Mike taking any kinds of lessons from a Catholic, in private.'

'You have to be careful,' the old woman said. 'I always tried to be careful where he was concerned. You were the one didn't keep close enough eye on him. Maybe if we'd both watched out, he wouldn't have gone wild like he did.'

'One last thing,' Chase said. 'And this might be kind of upsetting. If you don't feel like thinking about it, just say so.'

Anne Karnes looked at Glenda's bare legs, frowned, looked back at Chase. Harry stared over Chase's shoulder, like a glass-eyed mannequin.

Chase said, 'The funeral was Thursday, I believe. Did you notice anyone at the service whom you'd never seen before?'

'A lot of people,' Anne said.

'His friends mostly,' Harry said.

The old woman said, 'We hadn't met most of his friends. Once or twice he had someone here for an evening or overnight, but they were always giddy young men. I told him not to bring any more of them around if they couldn't sober themselves and act adult. And, of course, there were the girls that he – he'd known, girls from school and college.'

Chase described Judge as Brown had summed him

up. 'Was there anyone like that?'

'I wouldn't remember,' Anne said. 'There were so many.'

'Mr Karnes?'

'I don't recall him, no.'

The old man was crying. The tears hadn't come out of the corners of his eyes yet, but they hung there in fat droplets.

His wife saw his state and said, 'I guess I blame the boy too much. He wasn't a wicked boy. And you can't blame a child for its faults, can you? You have to go back to the parents, to us. If there was anything bad about Mikey, if he wasn't perfect, then it's because we weren't perfect ourselves. You can't raise a godly child when you have done wicked things yourself. It was us. Wasn't it, Dad?'

'Yes,' he said. 'We sinned, and we can't blame the boy.'

Chase was too depressed by them to remain any longer. He stood up abruptly and took Glenda's hand as she stood beside him. 'Thank you for your time and trouble,' he said. 'Sorry to have brought this all back into your minds again.'

'Not at all,' Mike's mother said. 'We're glad to help.'

Glenda spoke for the first time since they'd come into the living room. She picked up an evening paper and said, 'Is this today's paper?'

'Yes,' Anne said.

'If you've read it, I'd like to have it. I didn't get a chance to pick one up today.'

'Go ahead,' Anne said as she started them toward the hallway and the front door. 'Nothing good in it anyway.'

'You were in the army,' Harry Karnes called after them. He had turned sideways in his chair and was staring at Chase's open collar.

'Yes,' Chase said.

'I think that was what Mike needed. If we could have persuaded him to join the army and go to college later, maybe they'd have whipped him into shape, put sense into him. Maybe what he needed was a year or two over there, where you were.'

'That's the last thing he needed,' Chase said.

'Maybe, maybe not.'

'Take my word for it,' Chase said, the sympathy completely gone from him now, angry at the casualness with which the old man suggested sending his son to a living hell.

At the door, Mrs Karnes thanked him again and said she was happy to have met Glenda. She also said, 'Dear, aren't you cold in that little bit of a dress you're wearing?'

'Not at all,' Glenda said. 'It's a summer night.'

'Still and all –'

Glenda interrupted her. 'Besides, I'm a practicing nudist. I'd actually prefer going without any dress at all, if the law allowed.'

'Well, goodnight,' Anne Karnes said. She gave them a terribly strained smile and closed the door.

Chase said, 'You seem so soft and cuddly and sweet – until that acid streak shows up. You continue to amaze me.'

She took his arm as they walked to the car. 'Well, dammit, they made me sick. They aren't the least bit sorry for their son – only for themselves. And if he'd gone off to war and been killed that way, they'd have been proud as punch.'

'I know,' Chase said. 'I've seen it all before.' He put her in the car and went around, slid behind the wheel.

'This will interest you,' she said, opening the newspaper she had got from the Karneses' coffee table.

'What was that all about, by the way?'

She read the headline. 'Tavern owner found shot.'

'So?'

'It's Eric Blentz,' she said. 'They've got his picture on the front page.' She handed the paper to him.

Chase took the paper and read it in the glow of the streetlamp.

'Tell me,' she said.

'He was shot five times. Twice in the head and three times in the chest, at close range.'

'My God,' she said. She was shivering, and she reached automatically for a cigarette, which she lighted but did not smoke.

'He was found this afternoon at ten after twelve, by his sister.'

'That's the last evening edition,' Glenda said. 'It just made print, and it must be a small piece.'

'It is. Doesn't say much, except how he was found and where he lived – a town-house apartment on Galasio, out where the old golf course used to be.'

'I know the place,' she said. 'Shared walls in the town houses. And no one heard anything at all?'

'No.'

'Leads?'

'None here,' he said.

'What do you think, Ben?'

'It was Judge,' Chase said, convinced of it against his own will.

'You can't be positive.'

'But I am. When I left the tavern Saturday afternoon, I was fairly sure Blentz knew the man I'd described, but I couldn't see how to force it out of him. He must have tried to call Judge all Saturday evening while Judge was keeping a stakeout on your apartment. He wouldn't have got hold of him until Sunday afternoon at the earliest, perhaps late Sunday evening. He probably asked Judge to come see him at home this morning, and maybe he hinted about the reasons. He would have had time to realize who I was and to put the bits and pieces together. Maybe he wanted to blackmail Judge. He didn't look as if something like that would go against his grain.'

She crushed the cigarette in the ashtray. 'Can't even stand the smell of them burning any more.'

Chase said, 'I've been wondering why we haven't been followed or bothered all day. Now I think I know. If Blentz called him yesterday and asked to see him this morning, maybe hinted at the reason, Judge would have been pressed to stay up most of the night making plans. Perhaps the grenade was his last device before he heard from Blentz. Once he killed Blentz, he would have gone straight home to bed to catch up on his sleep. And I think I've read that psychotics sleep like dead dogs after a murder, exhausted by the emotional peak they've reached.'

'If he has slept all day,' Glenda said, 'he'll be up and around soon.'

'Yes,' Chase said. 'That's why we're going back to your place and locking up until morning. We can't get a list of physics tutors from the high school until nine o'clock or so. We might just as well shut down for the night.'

'I'm for going home,' she agreed. 'Being out in the open gives me the chills.'

'You're a nudist, remember? You're used to that sort of thing.'

'Those aren't the kind of chills I mean. Please, Ben, no jokes right now. I want to be taken home and fed some whisky until I fall asleep.'

'It's a deal,' he said.

No one followed them away from the house where Mike Karnes had once lived.

Thirteen

Tuesday morning after Glenda called in sick at work for the second day in a row, and after they had finished breakfast, Chase phoned the high school and represented himself as the father of a boy who needed a physics tutor to help sharpen him up for an advance placement test in college physics. The secretary he spoke with was pleasant and helpful. In ten minutes he had the names of four men who were interested in such moonlighting whenever it was available.

'Two of these were on the other list,' Glenda said. 'That means it has to be either Monroe Cullins or Richard Linski.'

'Not necessarily,' Chase said. 'These may not be the same men the high school was recommending a year ago.'

'We'll know shortly, won't we?'

He nodded and lifted the telephone again. He dialled Monroe Cullins' number and waited, wondering what

181

it would be like for Judge to realize, when he heard Chase's voice, that the tables had turned. Had *been* turned. This had been no accident of fate, but the result of hard work and more than a little cleverness.

No one answered Monroe Cullins' phone.

'It could be that Judge is here, watching the building.'

'And it could mean the guy is just out buying the newspaper or tending to an errand of some sort.'

'Try the other one.'

He put the phone down, looked at Richard Linski's number, picked the receiver up and dialled.

Again no one answered.

'Damn!' Glenda said.

Chase wiped his hands on his slacks, which she had pressed for him an hour earlier. 'We'll just have to wait. We'll try again, around noon, see if either one comes home for lunch.' His hands had left dark splotches of perspiration on his slacks.

Glenda passed the next hour trying to read, curled up in one of the velvet-covered easy chairs, her long legs tucked under her. Chase decided to read too, but found himself prowling the length of the bookshelves in the corridor, picking out one title after the other, only to replace it and go on. He felt as if he were looking for one special book, one certain topic, though he had nothing in mind. Once he thought he was looking for glass dogs that might be hidden behind the books.

At eleven the telephone rang.

'I'll get it,' Chase said.

'What if it isn't him?'

'Who else?'

'My mother, perhaps. Or someone from work.' She

got up and went to the phone and stood over it, watching it ring. She said, 'No, I'll have to get it myself.'

'Go on, then.'

She picked it up. 'Hello?' She smiled, placed a hand over the receiver. Her smile looked as if it had been hammered in a sheet of tin, stiff and beginning to rust. 'Mother,' she whispered.

He went back to the bookshelves and finally chose a picture history of erotic art. He didn't expect to be aroused just then, but at least there wasn't much reading to it.

Glenda's mother kept her on the phone fifteen minutes. When she hung up, she said, 'Mother wondered how ill I was.'

'How'd she know you called in sick?'

'Phoned me at work to tell me something; they told her.' She went back to her chair and picked up her book. 'Could we call those two now?

He looked at the wall clock just inside the hallway. 'Wait a little while yet.'

'I guess you're right,' she said. In the next half-hour she lighted and put out four cigarettes, though she smoked none of them.

Neither of the men was home when they called at noon. 'We'll try again at three,' Chase said.

They played cards for a while, took a bath together that did not lead anywhere erotic, watched a bit of afternoon television and tried reading again.

Neither of the men answered his phone at three.

Nor at five-thirty.

'I think I'll crack apart if we don't get hold of them soon,' Glenda said. 'I'm beginning to think crazy things – like maybe *both* of them are Judge.'

'I know what you mean,' Chase said. 'I was looking for glass dogs in your bookshelves a while ago.'

'Glass dogs?'

Before he could explain, the telephone rang. 'Your mother has already called, and it's too late to be someone from work.' He picked up the receiver and said hello.

'You can't stay inside forever,' Judge said. 'Sooner or later, you have to come out.'

'Why don't you come up and get us?' Chase asked. 'That would solve your problem.'

Judge laughed. 'You continually underestimate me – or were you only joking? Anyway, I only called to let you know I intend to take a break from the vigil, eat some supper and sleep a bit. You'll go unobserved for a while. It's perfectly safe to run out and stock up on milk and bread.' He started laughing again, and he required a long while to stop.

Chase said, 'You're pretty sure of yourself, aren't you?'

'And why not? I have all the time in the world; I can wait weeks for the proper moment.'

In the hours they had been waiting, he had had time to think about what to say to Judge if he should call again. Now it was almost like going through a printed script. 'Did you properly research Eric Blentz's past before you killed him?'

Judge was silent a moment, and when he did speak he sounded strained, on the verge of a scream. 'I knew him so well that I didn't need to do any research. He's deserved to die for years.'

'But especially since he discovered what you've

been up to.'

'I didn't kill him for personal reasons,' Judge said. 'You've got to understand that. He was a sinner, he deserved to die, I did the world a service by it.' His voice had deteriorated into an emotional garble. He hung up.

Chase said, 'Let's try those numbers again.'

'You think he called from home?'

'I think he's beyond taking precautions now.' He dialled Monroe Cullins' number. No one answered. Hesitantly, he dialled the number of Richard Linski and listened while it rang six times before it was answered. Chase let the man on the other end say hello half a dozen times, but he did not respond. When Linski broke the connection, Chase hung up.

'Well?' Glenda asked.

He said, 'It's him. Judge's real name is Richard Linski, the well-known physics tutor. We have him.'

Fourteen

Chase carried Glenda's overnight bag into the motel room and placed it at the foot of the double bed. He went back and closed the door, checked to see if the lock worked properly, slid the chain latch in place. The room was small, but clean and comfortable. There was no window in the bathroom, and the only window in the main room was filled by an air-conditioning unit.

'You're safe enough if you stay here,' he said.

'If I don't?'

'Glenda–'

She stood by the bathroom door, her hands fisted at her sides, very attractive in her anger. She had been very attractive for more than an hour. because she had been angry at him for that long. 'I know Linski's address as well as you, and I could get there right on your heels if I called a taxi as soon as you've gone.'

He went to her and put his hands on her shoulders. She did not resist, though she did not encourage him either.

'Glenda, you know he's dangerous, that he killed two people and that he threatened to kill us. I've been trained in self-defence, while you haven't. I've had field experience, while you haven't. It's as simple as that.'

'It's even simpler,' she said. 'Go to the police.'

'I told you I didn't want to yet.'

'*But why?*'

'I have to be sure this is Judge, that I'm not making a mistake somewhere. I wouldn't want to be laughed at again.'

She seemed to shrink, curling against him in defeat, but she continued to argue in a less strident tone of voice. 'Ben, you could call him on the telephone and confront him at a distance, couldn't you? You'd know soon enough that way.'

'I have to do this,' he said.

Although he was doing his best to try to convince her that his reasoning was sound, he was as unsure of his motives as she was. Everything she had said was true, but none of it helped to alleviate the intense need he felt to see Judge in person and to make the climax of this affair as sharp and sudden as possible.

'If Linski is guilty, his prints would match those on the knife that was used on Michael Karnes. An anonymous tip to the police. . .'

'I have to do this,' he repeated when she had run down like an old-time phonograph.

She leaned all her weight against him then, tired. 'Okay, okay. But I wish that I could have a least stayed home in my own apartment. Waiting here, in a strange place, makes it all the worse.'

'I've already explained why it has to be this way,' Chase said, gently massaging the back of her slim neck as he held her against him. 'He may have been lying when he said he was taking time off for supper and sleep. He may have been hoping to get me out of the apartment long enough to move in on you.'

'But he didn't bother us when we came out, and no one followed us here.'

'Still, I'm not taking chances with you. There's no way for him to know where you are now.' He kissed her once, only lightly, and broke the embrace. 'I have to get going if I want to catch him before he leaves home.'

'I'll wait for you,' she said reluctantly, having finally given in to him.

'You better, or I'll let the *Press-Dispatch* know you really haven't been sick the past two days.'

She did not smile at the joke, and he supposed that was understandable.

He unlocked the door and took the chain out of the slot, stepped outside onto the concrete promenade. He waited for her to close the door and to put both locks back in place, then left the motel in his Mustang.

Really alone for the first time in days, he found his mind wandering down avenues he had thus far managed to avoid. The argument with Glenda, however, had forced him to consider exactly what she meant to him and what losing her would do to his life. Before, he had *emotionally* accepted that such a loss would be greater than he could handle, but until this moment he had not intellectually faced the reasons *why* her death would destroy him. There was, naturally, the simple truth that he loved her as he never had loved another woman in his life. But men had lost love and had gone on to find happiness. It was not just that. He had to confront and accept the second reason her death must be prevented at all costs: if she died because of Judge, then she had indirectly died because of Chase, and she was his responsibility. If he hadn't come into her life, Judge wouldn't have known her. He had placed her in peril, and if he could not get her out of it, there was one more count of guilt to add to the list he already carried with him.

And that would mean insanity.

At a quarter past eight in the evening, Chase parked two blocks from Richard Linski's house and made the rest of the journey on foot, staying to the far side of the street. At the corner, half concealed by the public telephone booth, he looked the place over, setting it firmly in mind by daylight so that when he returned after dark, he would move more familiarly about it. It was a tidy little bungalow, second from the corner, and it was kept in good repair and appeared to have been painted recently: white with emerald-green trim and dark-green slate roof. It was set on one and a half lots, which were also well managed, the entire property ringed with waist-high hedges that were so even they might have been trimmed with the aid of a quality micrometer.

He turned and walked down the street that ran perpendicular to the one on which the bungalow faced, found the mouth of a narrow alleyway and entered it. He went far enough to be able to see the rear of Linski's house. A back porch, not so large as the Indian-style, wide-floored, roofed front veranda, led to a windowless back door. Windows flanked the door, and both were partially curtained in a cheery red and orange pattern.

Chase returned to the Mustang to wait until dark.

At first he tried to occupy himself with word games, then with the radio, but soon gave that up. He had been trying not to think about his impulsive decision to come here alone, for he did not want to puzzle out the nature of his reasons. He got out of the car and took a walk away from the bungalow, and in that manner he passed the time until half an hour after nightfall.

He approached the bungalow through the narrow alley and crouched by the thorny hedge where it parted for the entrance to the rear flagstone walk. The kitchen windows were lighted, though Chase could not see anyone in the room beyond them. He waited ten minutes, not thinking about anything, geared down and idling as he had learned to do in Nam before a crucial encounter, then he moved quickly forward, running silently on the lawn beside the walk, rushing from shrub to shrub with only a slight pause at each. When he reached the back porch, he remained crouched so that he was shielded from the windows by the wooden railing, the edge of the steps and the elevated floor of the porch itself, further cloaked with darkness.

Inside, a radio was playing instrumental versions of Broadway show tunes, between commercials delivered by a rather loud and unpleasant voice. It was the only sound.

Chase turned away from the house for a brief moment and surveyed the black lawn spread out behind him. At several points, lumps of shadow grew, shrubs and small trees, a miniature wheelbarrow planter full of wilted petunias. Nothing moved or reflected light.

When he was satisfied that he was alone, he looked back at the house and crept cautiously up the steps and onto the porch. There was a swing on the porch, a small cocktail table and two wicker chairs. A board squeaked under his foot and brought him to a standstill. He felt beads of sticky perspiration on his forehead and shivered uncontrollably as one of them trickled down his cheek, under his ear and down the side of his neck like a skittering cockroach. When he dared move again, the board squeaked as he stepped off it, but he was now convinced that Judge was not expecting him. He went to the wall of the house and pressed himself to it, between the window and the door.

He wished he had a gun.

What was he doing here without a gun?

Just checking things out. Get a look at Judge, at Linski, then run for it, be sure he matched his description, tie up that loose end, then call the cops.

He knew he was even lying to himself now.

Stooping low, he brought his face up to the window and peered into the tiny, bright kitchen. He saw a pine table and three chairs, a straw basket full of apples in the centre of the table, a refrigerator, an oven, all the other paraphernalia he might have seen in anyone's kitchen – but no Judge. Turning, he stepped past the door and bent at the second window. Here he was rewarded with the sight of a kitchen work area, canisters for flour and sugar and coffee, an instrument rack full of scoops and spoons and cooking forks, storage cabinets, a blender plugged into a wall outlet – but no Judge. Unless Linski was standing directly behind the door, trying not to be seen – an unlikely possibility – he was somewhere else in the house.

Chase pulled open the screen door, and winced as it made a high, sweet singing noise which seemed to cut throught the quiet night air like a gunshot, a sure alarm.

No one came to investigate.

CHASE

The music on the radio had covered him, more likely than not.

He put his hand on the doorknob and slowly turned it as far as it would go, took a last deep breath to help quiet his nerves and pressed the door open. It was not locked. He stepped quickly into the house, looked around at the empty kitchen and closed the door after him. The hinges were well oiled; the door did not make a sound.

For the first time since he had conceived of this foray, Chase was conscious of his nakedness, of the fact that he had come unarmed, and he felt his neck aching as it had after Judge had taken a bead on it with his pistol and then missed. He considered trying the drawers in the cupboard by the sink and securing a sharp knife, then dismissed the idea. For one thing, he would be certain to make considerable noise pulling open drawers full of silverware, more noise than the violins and trumpets could drown. Secondly, he would be wasting precious time in such a search, minutes during which Judge might step into the kitchen after a glass of water and come upon him, negating any advantage of surprise that he might otherwise possess. Finally, there would be far more satisfaction in taking Richard Linski with his own two hands instead of with an impersonal weapon.

Of course, he would not actually attempt to apprehend Judge – unless he was seen and had no other choice – for that was the job of the police. Ideally, he would come upon Judge asleep in the bedroom, make a quick identification without waking him and beat it the hell out of there. Ideally, there would be no trouble.

Another lie.

He paused at the archway between the kitchen and the dining room, for there were no lights where he was going next, just what spilled from the kitchen and living room. In a few minutes he had assured himself that no one was hiding by the heavy pine hutch or the dining table, and he crossed swiftly to the open doorway that led to the main living room. Here the floor was carpeted in shag pile, softening the sound of footsteps.

He stood at the threshold of the front room, letting his eyes adjust to the brighter light.

Someone coughed. A man.

In Nam, when a mission was especially tense, he had been able to devote his mind to its completion with a singleness of purpose that he had never achieved on anything else in his life, to become almost obsessed with the chore at hand. He wanted to be as brisk and clean and quick about this as he had been about those missions, but he was bothered by thoughts of Glenda sitting all alone in that strange motel room, waiting for him to return. . .

He was evading the moment, he knew. He could not hesitate; he must get on with it.

He flexed his hands and drew a slow breath, preparing himself for the fight, even though he was sure there would not be one.

Another lie.

The smart thing to do, the civilized thing to do, was to turn around right now, cross the darkened dining room as quietly as possible, cross the kitchen and leave by the back door and call the police.

He stepped into the living room.

A man sat in a large white recliner chair close to the television set, a newspaper on his lap. He wore tortoise-shell reading glasses pushed far down on his thin, straight nose, and he was humming a sprightly tune which Chase could not identify. He was reading the comics.

For a moment Chase was certain that he had made a dangerous mistake, for he had never anticipated this: a psychotic killer engaged in a pastime so mundane, engrossed in the latest exploits of Snoopy and Charlie Brown, B.C. and Broom Hilda. Then the man looked up, taking on the cliché pose of total surprise: eyes wide, mouth slightly open, face gone hard and white. And Chase saw that the man fit Judge's description to a detail. Tall. Blond. Harsh about the face, with thin lips and a long, straight nose.

'Richard Linski?' Chase asked.

The man in the chair seemed frozen into place, perhaps a mannequin propped there to distract Chase while the real Judge, the real Richard Linski, crept up on him from behind. The illusion was so complete that for a few seconds Chase almost turned around to see if the dining room was empty behind him or if his fears were correct.

The man in the chair was gripping the pages of the newspaper so hard they might have been made of steel.

'Judge?' Chase asked.

'You,' the man whispered.

He wadded the steel pages in his hands and came out of the easy chair as if he had sat upon a tack.

'Yes,' Chase said, suddenly calmed, 'it's me.'

Fifteen

Although Chase had learned the value of concentrating exclusively on the mission at hand during his tour in Vietnam, he had never been one for psyching himself before an operation. Too often the unit never encountered the Cong they had been told were out there, and the mission ended without a shot fired. The men who had worked themselves up, put themselves on edge, on the theory they would perform better under pressure, were left frustrated and had no acceptable outlets for their nervous energy. These were the ones, most often, who worked off their tension on innocent civilians, hyped into a plastic paranoia, into a period of schizophrenia where the sound of gunfire and the odour of burning buildings was like a soporific to lead them back down the scale of frenzy to a point where they could regain control of themselves. Chase had let himself get carried away like that only one time, and the operation had been a disaster that haunted him ever afterward.

Now, as he faced Judge at last, his ability to control himself and to keep calm proved to be valuable. The confrontation did not immediately progress to violence, as he had envisioned it might.

'What are you doing here?' Judge asked.

He had backed away from the white chair, toward the television set. His hands were out at his sides, the fingers working as if he were searching for something to use as a bludgeon.

'What do you think?' Chase asked. He started slowly toward Linski, gauging the man's retreat.

'You don't *belong* here.'

Chase said nothing.

'This is my *home*,' Judge said.

When Judge came up against the television set, Chase stopped ten feet away from him, sizing him up, waiting for the proper moment. He wished it had not come to this, that he could have gotten a good look at Judge without being seen himself.

Still lying.

'Nobody else belongs here,' Judge said. 'This is my home, and I want you out of it.' He sounded properly irate, except for a quaver in his voice.

'No,' Chase said.

'Get out!'

'No.'

'Goddamn you!' Judge said.

He was standing with his hands out to his sides like wings, and he was beginning to weep. The tears slipped out of the corners of his eyes and hung on his cheeks from wet threads.

Chase said, 'I want you to walk slowly toward the telephone on that stand, and I want you to call the police.'

But even as he said it, he knew that was not going to be possible.

'I won't do it,' Judge said.

'I think you will.'

'You can't make me do it,' Judge said. As he spoke, he began to turn, and on the last word he grabbed something from the top of the television set.

Too late, Chase saw that it was the pistol. He did not see how he could have overlooked something like that. He must have gotten far more out of practice than he had thought. Or he had chosen to ignore it for some reason that escaped his conscious mind. He stepped forward as Judge brought the weapon up, the grey tube of the homemade silencer still attached, but he did not move quite fast enough. The bullet took him in the left shoulder and twisted him sideways, off balance and into the floor lamp.

He fell over, taking the lamp with him. Both bulbs smashed when they struck the floor, plunging the room into near total darkness that was relieved only by the weak light from distant streetlamps that managed to filter through the heavy drapes.

'Are you dead?' Judge asked.

His shoulder felt as if a nail had been driven into it, and his entire arm was numb. He could feel blood running down his side, but he did not want to reach over and explore the seriousness of the wound – first, because he did not want to know if it was a bad one, and second, because he preferred that Judge think he was either dead or dying.

'Chase?'

Chase waited.

Judge stepped away from the television, bent forward

as he tried to make out Chase's body in the jumble of shadows and furniture. Chase could not tell for certain, but he thought the man was holding the pistol straight out in front of him, like a teacher holding a pointer toward the blackboard. That was good. That made him more vulnerable

'Chase?'

Chase forced his wounded arm off the floor as if it were a dead weight of some size, bent it at the elbow and laid the palm flat against the carpet as he had already done with his other hand. He felt weak, shaking all over, his stomach like a knotted rag, perspiration pouring from his face and along the length of his spine. He knew that most of the problem was shock, and that when he made his move he would have the necessary strenth to overcome that.

'How's our hero now?' Judge asked. Apparently he had stopped crying, for there was low, pleased laughter in his voice. 'Are you planning on getting your name in the paper again?' He laughed out loud now and took another step forward.

Chase pushed himself up and launched forward at Judge's feet, ignoring the scream of pain in his shoulder. He came in under the barrel of the pistol that Judge still held out before him like an old woman searching for a burglar.

The pistol fired, the *whoosh* of the silencer clearly audible in such close quarters; the bullet shattered something at the other end of the room but came nowhere near Chase.

They went backward into the television set, which Judge caught with his hips and knocked from its stand. It struck the wall and then the floor with two solid thumps, though the screen did not break. Unable to complete the backward fall because of the obstacles, Judge was overbalanced the other way and crashed down on Chase. The pistol flew from his hand and rattled against the wooden feet of the easy chair. He tried to scramble after it, but Chase had a good hold on him and did not intend to let go.

Chase rolled and carried Judge over with him, assumed the top position and quickly drove his knee into Judge's crotch. Linski cried out, though his scream settled abruptly into a strained gasp of pain. He attempted to heave up and throw Chase loose, but he could not manage more than a weak, fluttered protest. He was crying again.

Chase's wounded shoulder throbbed from his having rolled on it, and it felt as if the bones must have rotted beneath the flesh. Despite the pain, he reached forward with both hands, found the correct pressure points on Judge's neck and bore down with his thumbs long enough to be certain that the killer was unconscious. When he stood up, swaying back and forth like a drunkard, Linski remained on the floor, his hands still spread at his sides, now like a bird that had fallen out of the sky and had broken its back on a thrust of rock.

Chase wiped at his face, flicked the sweat from his fingers. His stomach, knotted only minutes ago, had loosened too quickly, like a greased rope curling on itself, and he felt as if he might be sick. He could not afford that luxury.

Outside, a car full of shouting teenagers went by, screeched at the corner, sounded its horn and peeled off with a squeal of rubber.

Chase stepped across Richard Linski's body and

looked out the window. There was no one in sight. The lawn was dark. The sounds of the struggle had not carried any distance.

He turned away from the glass and listened to Linski's breathing. It was shallow but steady.

Chase crossed the room to the other floor lamp, tripped over an ottoman on the way, found the lamp and switched it on.

He looked at his shoulder, probed the hole in the fleshy part of his biceps. As far as he could tell, the bullet had passed straight through. He could look at it in a moment, under stronger light, as soon as he secured Judge.

He could also call the police. In a little while. After he had taken care of a couple of loose ends that yet remained.

Sixteen

In the bathroom, Chase stripped off his blood-soaked shirt and dropped it in the sink. He washed the wound and tested the flow of blood, sopping it up with a washcloth until it was not bleeding dangerously any more. He located the alcohol in the medicine chest and poured half a bottle over and into the hole, was nearly knocked down by the rush of stinging pain that exploded in the wake of the fluid. For a while he bent over the sink, staring into the mirror, watching the circles under his eyes grow darker, the whites of his eyes more bloodshot. When he felt he could move again, he found gauze pads and soaked one of them in Merthiolate. He slapped that over the wound, covered it with more clean pads, then wound wide-band adhesive tape over the entire mess. It wasn't professional, but it would keep him from leaking blood over everything.

In the bedroom, he took one of Judge's shirts from the closet and struggled into it. If their fight had been now instead of ten minutes ago, he would surely have lost, for his shoulder and back were beginning to stiffen considerably.

In the kitchen, he found a large plastic garbage sack and brought it to the bathroom. He dropped his bloody shirt, the bloody towel and washcloth into it. He used tissues and wads of toilet paper to wipe up the sink and the mirror, threw those in the bag when he was done with them. Standing in the doorway, he looked the bathroom over, decided there was no trace of what he had done there, turned off the light and closed the door.

Judge's second shot had missed Chase, but it had thoroughly smashed a three-foot-square ornamental mirror that had hung on the wall above the bar at the far end of the living room. Bits of glass lay over everything within a six-foot radius. In five minutes he had picked up all the major shards, though hundreds of tiny slivers still sparkled in the nap of the carpet and in the upholstery of nearby chairs.

He was considering this problem when Judge awoke. He went to the chair in the middle of the living room, where he had tied the killer with clothesline he had found in the kitchen. It was a straight-backed, unpadded, armless chair that provided a number of rungs and slats to snake the rope through. Judge twisted and tried to break free, but soon saw there was no hope of that.

Chase said, 'Where is your vacuum sweeper?'

'What?' Judge was still groggy.

'Vacuum sweeper.'

'What you want that for?'

Chase slapped him hard with his good hand.

'In the cellarway,' Judge said.

He brought the sweeper back, plugged it in and picked

up every piece of shattered mirror that caught his eye. Fifteen minutes later, satisfied, he put the sweeper away again, just as he had found it.

'What are you up to?' Judge asked. He was still trying at his ropes, as though not convinced it was hopeless.

Chase did not answer. He picked up the television and replaced it on its stand, plugged it in and tried it. It still worked. There was a situation comedy playing, one of those in which the father is always an idiot and the mother is little better. The kids are cute monsters.

Next he picked up the floor lamp he had fallen over and examined the metal shade. It was dented, but there was no way to tell that the dent was new. He unscrewed the damaged light bulbs, and along with the larger scraps of the broken mirror, threw them in the plastic garbage bag on top of the bloody shirt and towel. He used the pages of a magazine to scoop up the smaller pieces, and threw those and the magazine into the garbage bag.

'Where are your spare light bulbs kept?' Chase asked Linski.

'I'm not telling you.'

'You will, eventually.'

Judge remained silent, glowering at Chase. Chase noticed that just as intended, there were no bruises on the man's throat where Chase's thumbs had dug into him. The pressure had been too pinpointed and too quick to seriously hurt tissue.

Chase back-handed Linski across the face, three times.

Linski said, 'In the kitchen, under the sink, behind the box of laundry detergent. What are you trying to prove with all this?'

Chase did not answer. He found the bulbs and screwed

two new ones into the lamp. They worked when he switched them on.

In the kitchen again, he got a bucket of water, soap, ammoniated cleanser and a carton of milk – his mother's favourite spot remover – from the refrigerator. In the living room, he used a rag and a succession of the substances to get the worst of the blood spots out of the carpet. The faint brown stains that remained were easily hidden by the long nap of the shag rug.

He put everything away again and threw the rag into the garbage bag with the other things.

After that, he stood in the centre of the room and slowly examined all of it for traces of the fight. The blood had been mopped up, the furniture righted, the broken glass thrown out. The only thing that might draw anyone's suspicion was the soot-ringed, pale square where the ornate mirror had hung.

Chase pulled the two picture hangers out of the wall; they left two small nail holes behind. He used a handful of paper towels to wipe away most of the dirty ring, successfully blending the lighter and darker portions of the wall. It was still obvious that something had hung there, though one might now think it had been removed several months ago.

Judge watched all of this without asking any more questions.

Chase came back to him and sat down on the arm of the easy chair. He said, 'I have some questions to ask you.'

'Go to hell,' Judge said.

Chase hit him hard. He said, 'First of all, did you really intend to kill Louise Allenby, or just Mike?'

'Both of them,' Judge said.

'Why?'

'I've explained all of that.'

'Explain it again.' Chase's arm felt as if it were falling off, but the severe pain kept him alert.

'They were fornicators,' Linski said. 'I followed them and watched them until I knew for sure.'

'And why should that bother you? Because Mike should have been your lover?'

Perhaps Judge realized that there was no way out, no hope of continuing to hide anything. He no longer bothered to deny his sexual proclivities. He said, 'He was a beautiful boy, and he seemed to like me. But I made a major mistake in approaching him. It became almost an obsession with me, his youthfulness, the grace in him that older men soon lose, his smile, his enthusiasm, his vital energy. I should not have started any of it.'

'And that's why you killed him.'

'No,' Judge said. 'It started out because of that, but it grew into something much more important.' There was a peculiar spark of interest in his eyes, a morbid excitement. 'When I followed him, I saw what loose morals he had – and what loose morals most of his generation has. I was negatively impressed by the rutting that went on in the park on Kanackaway, for instance. It soon became obvious to me that unless something was done to set an example for this generation, the country would one day decline as Rome declined.'

Chase felt tired. He had been hoping for something more than this, something original and fresh. Madmen, he supposed, always clung to the same stale ideas, though. He said, 'And you would single-handedly bring about a change in the morals of all young people – just by showing them what was liable to happen to – fornicators.'

'Yes,' Judge said. 'I know that I'm tainted myself.

CHASE

Don't think I'm blind to my own weaknesses. But by embarking on a crusade of this sort. I could surely pay penance for my own sins and contribute positively to the Christian standards of the community.'

Chase laughed.

'I see nothing funny,' Judge said.

'I do,' Chase said. 'You ought to meet Mike Karnes's parents. Have you ever met them?'

'No,' Judge said, perplexed.

Chase was still laughing, but he realized it was not healthy laughter, too forced and tight for that. He stopped and sat there for a moment, regaining his composure. He said, 'What about Blentz?'

'I knew him once – in the Biblical sense.'

'He was your lover?' Chase asked.

'Yes. But he was petty and nasty, and he threatened to expose me for what I was. He didn't care about his own involvement. He said he wouldn't care if the whole city knew.'

'He had the right attitude,' Chase said.

'Exposing your own sin, revelling in it? That is a healthy attitude?'

'Something like homosexuality is only a sin if you want to think of it that way,' Chase said. 'To other people, it's just another way of facing the world.'

'You're corrupted, like everyone else,' Judge said. 'At least I recognize it for the weakness it is.'

'How long ago were you and Blentz lovers?'

Judge said, 'Two years ago, maybe longer. We saw each other occasionally since then, but not in anything but a social context.'

'When did he call to tell you I'd been around asking questions?'

206

'Sunday afternoon. He wanted to see me Monday morning, and he made the mistake of hinting that he knew what I'd done.'

'Why wouldn't he have gone straight to the police?'

Judge strained at his ropes, then sank back, gasping for breath. When he could speak easily again, he said. 'He wanted money. The same way he threatened to expose me two years ago, same payoff.'

'I'd think he would have more money than you,' Chase said.

'He gambled. When he saw this chance, he took it.'

'You shot him with that gun?'

'Yes.'

Chase said, 'Where'd you get the grenade?'

Judge seemed to brighten for a moment. 'I'm a major in the reserves. When we had manoeuvres this summer, it was a simple matter to lift one of them from the metal storage chests they keep them in. I thought it might come in handy, and it almost did.'

Chase found paper and pen in the dining-room desk, picked up a large coffee-table picture book on Africa and brought everything back to Linski. He placed the book on Linski's lap, the paper on the book, the pen on the paper. He said, 'I've tied your hands separately. I'm going to loosen your right hand and hold onto it with this rope. I'll dictate a confession; you'll write it. If you try anything, I'll beat the shit out of you. Do you believe that?'

'I believe it,' Judge said.

Chase dictated the confession, saw that it was done properly, retied Judge's arm. He put the book on the coffee table again, put the pen in the desk.

'You must be thrilled,' Judge said. 'I don't know how

you found me, but it must be a clever story that'll make nice front-page reading.'

'I won't let it get into the paper,' Chase said. 'At least not my part in it.'

'Bullshit, Chase. Pure bullshit. You know there's no way you can keep it off page one. Even if you won't admit it, you must know you're a publicity monger, a cheap little tin war hero who has had his taste of glory and can't break the habit.'

'No,' Chase said. 'You don't understand at all.'

'Get a kick out of being a celebrity, do you? You killed all those women and children–'

'Not me alone.'

'– and now every time you get your picture in the paper, you're trading on that kind of 'heroism.' Medal of Honor winner. What a laugh that is, Chase. You're disgusting.'

'I didn't want the medal,' Chase said. He did not know why he had to defend himself to Judge of all people.

'Sure.'

'That's the truth.'

'But you took it and the car and the awards dinner.'

'Because that was the quickest way to get it over with and settle down again. If I'd refused any of those things, the curiosity of the press would have been ten times worse.'

'Rationalization, that's all.'

'It isn't!' Chase shouted. 'Dammit, I don't want to be a hero. I just want to live, the best that I can, as happy as I can. I'm not a hero at all.'

'Why don't you tell that to the press?'

Chase stood up, agitated. He did not want to go on in this vein any longer. He said, 'Did you really intend to kill Glenda?'

'The blonde slut you're with?'

'Glenda,' Chase repeated.

'Of course,' Judge said. 'She's a fornicator, just like you, just like the Allenby girl. And I still may kill you, all of you, bring you the proper judgment.'

'Oh?'

'You don't think they'll send me to prison, do you? They'll sock me away in an institution and give me psychiatric care. Though if they try to give me Dr Cauvel, I'll scream bloody murder.' He laughed until he choked, blinked tears from his eyes. 'I'll get out again, maybe not for ten years or fifteen. But they won't keep me until I die.' He looked at the paper lying by his feet. 'Besides, you've forced a confession from me. That might be just enough to cause a mistrial, if it's introduced as evidence.'

Chase picked up the pistol which he had placed on the television set. 'You made the silencer yourself?'

'Yes,' Judge said. 'It wasn't that difficult. A piece of pipe the proper diameter, the shop tools at the school where I teach – presto!' He smiled at Chase. 'That would make a good picture for the front page, you standing over me with the murder weapon in your hand, triumphant and glorious.'

Chase slapped him hard with the back of his hand. When Judge's mouth fell, he jammed the silenced barrel between the man's teeth and pulled the trigger. Once.

He dropped the gun and turned away from the dead man, walked into the hall and opened the bathroom door. He put up the lid of the toilet bowl, and after a few moments, vomited into the water. He remained on his knees for a long time, coughing up bile before he could control spasms that racked him. He flushed the toilet three times, put the lid down and sat on it, wiping at the cold sweat on his face.

It was done.

No more lies.

Having won the Congressional Medal of Honor, the most sacred and jealously guarded award the country had, he had only wanted to return to the attic room in Mrs Fiedling's house and take up his penitence again. They had not allowed him that much.

Then he met Glenda, and things changed. There was no question about returning to the hermetic way of life, sealed off from experience. All that he wanted now was a quietude, a chance for their love to develop, a normal life. Cauvel, the police and Richard Linski had not allowed him that. The press, if it were found that he had solved the case himself, would not allow him that either.

He had known, without admitting it to himself, from the moment he had decided to come out here on his own, that he intended to kill Linski in just such a fashion. While he cleaned up all signs of the fight in the living room, he knew it. But he had not faced up to it until he pulled the trigger.

Examining his conscience, he felt no guilt. This was different from the women in the tunnel. They had done nothing to him, had offered no genuine threat to his peace. Judge, however, brought an end to hopes of peace.

Chase rose and went to the sink. He rinsed his mouth out until the bad taste was gone, then returned to the commode, sat down and tried to think the rest of it through.

He felt no guilt, because other people had driven him

into a corner – and permitted him to escape by using the deadly skills the army had taught him. He had won by their rules. He was sorry for what he'd done, but the guilt was reserved for those Vietnamese women who would live as a part of him until he died. He had subconsciously ignored the gun on the television set, he now saw, taking the wound in his shoulder as further punishment and reason to act. Besides, Richard Linski had been as much a victim of national hypocrisy as he had himself. Play it rough in war and in business at home. That was the way of the nation, and he had become an acolyte to the religion.

He no longer had to be a hero.

He got up and left the bathroom.

In the front room, he untied Richard Linski's body and let it sprawl on the floor. He wiped the chair with wet paper towels until there was no blood on it, replaced it at the dining-room table, then put the towels in the plastic garbage bag.

When he considered the pistol, he realized there would be three slugs missing from the clip, but he could do nothing about that. It was no proof that Judge had shot at anyone or that he had not killed himself. He wiped the gun with a towel he had got from the linen closet and pressed Judge's hand around it to leave unmistakable prints.

With the pistol out of the way, he searched for the two slugs which Judge had expended earlier. He found one embedded in the baseboard, and he dug it out without leaving a very noticeable mark. The other was behind the portable bar under the spot where the mirror had rested. He dug it out along with a large piece of glass that he had overlooked the first time.

Using the same towel, he decided to begin wiping

everything he had touched, but brought himself up short at that. There might be a good many fingerprints on things as it was, enough to mask his own a bit. If the police found the doorknob wiped clean, however, they'd not believe the suicide angle for a minute. He put the towel in the plastic sack.

It was a quarter to twelve when he reached the Mustang and put the garbage bag in the trunk. He got in, started the engine and drove down the street past Linski's bungalow. The lights were burning. They would burn all night.

On the way back to the motel, he began to think about Glenda and about taking her to bed again, soon, within the hour. This time, he felt almost certain, there would be no inability on his part. That thought, combined with the knowledge that Judge was out of their lives for good, served to liberate his spirit, loosen one bond after another until he felt as if he were soaring. Giddy, he considered how soon he should ask her to marry him; he wanted her as a wife, more than he had wanted anything.

He had not forgotten Operation Jules Verne. It was just that he had come to see that he was as much a victim of his society as the Vietnamese women had been victims of theirs. Guilt should be tempered with hope and happiness, even for him.

He thought about Glenda again, pictured her as his wife, liked the picture. In a few years they might even have a baby. Just one child. He didn't want her to become a baby machine. And if it were a boy, none of Them would touch him, none of Them would take him away when he turned eighteen and teach him to kill. Society had taught Chase how to play tough, and he would use every trick he had learned to protect his own.

CHASE

She was waiting in the room, sitting on the bed with the television whispering at her. When he knocked, she unlatched and unchained the door, looked out warily, then grinned.

'What happened?' she asked as she welcomed him inside.

He began to unbutton her blouse, and the sense of capability did not leave him. He was shaking a little, but he did not think she would notice. He said, 'He killed himself.'

'*What?*'

'When I got there, I took my time sneaking into the place, wormed my way to the living room – and found him dead. He'd left a suicide note.'

'But what took you so long?'

'I didn't build up the nerve to go into the house until after ten. When I found him, I had to sit down and think it out. I wiped my prints off the doorknob and everything I touched, then took my time getting out of there in case someone might be watching from another house.'

'You're sure he's dead?'

'Yes.'

She came against him, her hand on his arm, directly over the lump of his makeshift bandage. 'What's this?'

'I fell and cut myself.'

She helped him take his shirt off, and she undid the bandage. 'Cut yourself on what?'

'A broken mirror,' he said, feeling sick. 'I broke a mirror in Linski's place and cut my arm.'

'Come into the bathroom,' she said.

It had stopped bleeding and was crusted black and

ugly. She bathed it tenderly and used one of the pillowcases to make clean strip bandages. 'We should see a doctor about this.'

'It'll be all right,' he said. He took her head in his hands when she had finished tending him, and said, 'Glenda, will you marry me?'

'You're in shock,' she said. 'Don't propose marriage when you're not clear-headed.'

'If you don't answer me now,' he said, 'I'm afraid I'm going to start screaming and be unable to stop.'

She smiled, but quickly saw that he was serious. She said, 'You haven't said you love me.'

'Haven't I? My own stupidity. I do, and you know that I do. And I also should tell you that from now on I think I can also love you in the physical sense as well.' He smiled at her. 'Marry me?'

She stood and unhooked her bra, stepped out of her skirt and panties.

'Please answer me,' he said.

'I am answering you,' she said. 'I'm answering you in the most positive way I can think of. Let's go to bed, darling.'

Later, very much later, as they lay side by side on the motel bed, she said, 'I want to pick up your things tomorrow and move you in with me.'

'What will your mother think?'

'She'll have to accept the fact that I'm a grown girl. Besides, you've said you'll marry me rather than live in sin.'

'It's a deal,' Chase said. 'First thing in the morning; I don't have much to be moved.' He thought that now he even had enough determination to tell Mrs Fiedling to button the neck of her damn housedress.